"Is there someone else?" Leanne's fingers moved sensuously up and down Dixon's neck.

"No." Dixon closed her eyes as Leanne's knee gently but insistently pushed between her legs. Dixon tried to recall the last time she had made love. Too long, her throbbing body yelled back.

"I'm not looking for a lifetime commitment. Let's enjoy what the moment has to offer," Leanne said, unbuttoning Dixon's shirt.

In one deft movement Dixon's bra was loose and on the floor beside her shirt. The breeze from the air conditioner caused her already taut nipples to tighten more. Dixon opened her eyes to find Leanne staring at her hungrily.

"If you don't want this, all you have to do is say stop," Leanne said.

Visit

Bella Books

at

BellaBooks.com

or call our toll-free number

1-800-729-4992

Whispers
in the Wind

frankie j. jones

Bella
BOOKS

2005

Bella Books, Inc.
P.O. Box 10543
Tallahassee, FL 32302

First published 1999 by Naiad Press

Printed in the United States of America on acid-free paper
First Edition

Editor: Lila Empson
Cover designer: Sandy Knowles

ISBN 1-59493-037-6

To Peggy
Every day with you is a new adventure

Acknowledgments

Thanks to Peggy J. Herring for giving me the greatest feedback any author could ever hope to receive—honesty. I would also like to thank Sara Al-Jundi, for all of her help in describing the Guadalupe Mountains, and Martha Cabrera, for reading the manuscript and offering much-needed advice.

About the Author

Frankie J. Jones is the author of *Rhythm Tide*, *Whispers in the Wind*, *Captive Heart*, *Room for Love*, *Midas Touch* and *Survival of Love*. She enjoys fishing, traveling, outdoor photography and rummaging through flea markets in search of whimsical salt and pepper shakers.

Authors love to hear from their readers. You may contact Frankie through Bella Books at fjjones@bellabooks.com, or directly at FrankieJJones@aol.com.

CHAPTER ONE

Dixon Hayes pushed the last rock into place. "That should keep the tent anchored against the wind," she said, and brushed the dust from her hands. She straightened up to stretch the kinks out of her back and gazed at the towering view offered at the Pine Springs Campground of the Guadalupe Mountains National Park.

"You know, Dixon, there are people who manage to go on vacation without taking half of their household with them," Elizabeth Colter groaned, arriving with the last of their camping gear from Dixon's truck.

After setting the load of bags on the picnic table, she dropped into a lawn chair. "I'm exhausted."

Dixon was relieved that Elizabeth was beginning to talk. She had been unusually silent during the long drive from San Antonio. Dixon attributed it to stress.

Elizabeth was a high school history teacher. It often seemed like Elizabeth spent more time fighting with the school board and administrators for new textbooks and other necessary supplies than she did teaching. Since football was the district's major focus, the other departments were always short of funds. To compensate for the material items she couldn't provide her students, Elizabeth spent much of her spare time offering them emotional support.

"I brought that stuff because I know how you can't survive without all the comforts of home," Dixon teased. "When I go camping I only take the bare necessities."

Elizabeth shuddered. "Someday we're going to go where I want. I'm going to haul you away on a vacation that involves room service and real beds. We'll spend hours in museums and libraries." It was Dixon's turn to shudder. The look of total horror on her face caused Elizabeth to burst into laughter. "Dixon, being with you keeps me sane."

The sun was slipping below the horizon, splashing the sky with glorious multicolored streaks of red, blue, pink, and purple. The two women, absorbed in the spectacular array, stood on a ledge high above their campsite.

Dixon felt the familiar tightness in her throat and

the touch of euphoria that always accompanied this breathtaking display.

"It is beautiful up here," Elizabeth admitted, gazing at the vista before them.

"I've never seen a place more beautiful. Come on over here." Dixon held out her hand to Elizabeth, who stood well away from the edge.

"I'm fine right here," Elizabeth assured her.

"You'll be perfectly safe."

"I can see everything I want to from here, thank you."

"But you're missing the great view down below. I can see our tent," Dixon said and craned her neck farther over the ledge.

"Dixon, I've already seen the tent, and honestly, it's not much to look at."

Dixon, knowing Elizabeth wasn't fond of heights, shrugged. "All right, but you don't know what you're missing." When Elizabeth still didn't budge, Dixon sighed. Sometimes Elizabeth's overcautious nature irritated her. "Come on. Let's head back to camp before it gets any darker."

They approached a particularly steep slope, and Dixon reached back to offer Elizabeth a hand just as Elizabeth's feet slipped. Dixon caught her and instinctively pulled Elizabeth's short, compact body to her. The physical jolt of contact sent Dixon's heart into a new biorhythm. Even though Elizabeth was a lesbian, she had regretfully broken the news to Dixon several years ago that she only thought of her as a very special friend. Devastated, Dixon had fled to California for two years before deciding that friendship was better than nothing. Over the years, she had managed to put her feelings for Elizabeth into a

3

tightly sealed emotional pocket. Only on rare and unguarded moments did a touch or glance from Elizabeth break the seal and allow some of the pain to slip through.

They had met nine years earlier when Dixon was still working as a photographer for a San Antonio newspaper.

She had been sent by the paper to get photos of an archaeological team that was searching for the fabled lost treasure of the Alamo.

Elizabeth was there with her history students observing the dig. When Dixon had first noticed her, Elizabeth had been deeply engrossed in telling her students about the history of the area prior to the famed battle. Dixon found herself attracted to the petite, intense woman with the cool, jade-green eyes.

After several minutes of following the group around, Dixon had introduced herself and had ended up with more shots of Elizabeth's class than of the dig site.

Unable to stop thinking about her, Dixon had called Elizabeth the next day and invited her to lunch. Their conversation had come easily. As the weeks slipped by, a strong friendship formed between them, one that over the years managed to survive the major obstacle of Dixon's attraction.

She could feel Elizabeth trembling in her arms and wanted to believe it was a reaction to being near her, but she knew the slide was responsible.

"Hey," Dixon said, holding her tighter and pulling her head to her shoulder. She tried to ignore the sparks of desire that struck her as her fingertips stroked Elizabeth's short, coarse hair. "You're all right. It was just a little slip. I have you now."

"I'm three months pregnant," Elizabeth blurted into Dixon's neck.

Dixon felt the verbal blow land squarely in her solar plexus. "You're what?" She was too stunned to move.

"Damn. This wasn't exactly how I planned on telling you," Elizabeth said. She pulled away, careful not to make eye contact with Dixon. "Let's go back to the camp and talk about it there. It's getting dark fast."

Too stunned to argue, Dixon took the flashlight from her pocket and started down the path. Sheer instinct guided Dixon back to the campsite. She was too shocked to pay attention where she was going. Anger born of fear began to consume her as they walked.

Elizabeth had got pregnant by artificial insemination two years earlier and had almost died from complications that ended in a miscarriage. Elizabeth's sister, Jennifer, and Dixon had sat by her side for hours, not knowing whether she would live or die. For three long, agonizing months afterward, Elizabeth had been lost in a world of grief. Since the miscarriage she hadn't mentioned trying to get pregnant again, and Dixon had assumed Elizabeth had given up on the idea.

When they reached the campsite, Dixon lit the lantern and started digging through the boxes looking for food for their dinner. Why hadn't Elizabeth told her she was trying to get pregnant? After all, they were best friends. She grabbed a can of chili.

"Dixon, come over here and sit down. I want to talk to you," Elizabeth begged.

"I'm hungry."

"I know you're angry that I didn't tell you I was trying to get pregnant again, but I was afraid you'd be upset and try to talk me out of it."

"It's obviously nothing to me." Dixon struggled with the can opener, which blurred through her tears. For some reason the opener kept slipping off the rim of the can. The third time it slipped, she grabbed the can of chili and hurled it into the darkness. It slammed into a tree with a sharp thud.

"Don't," Elizabeth said, hugging Dixon to her. "It won't be like before." She clasped Dixon's hands to her abdomen. "We're both okay. I've been to see my doctor, and she's assured me that everything's okay." She soothed Dixon's hair back. "I was careless before. If anything goes wrong, I promise I'll . . . I'll take the necessary precautions. I want this baby, but I won't jeopardize my life again." She wiped the tears from Dixon's face. "I pinkie swear." She extended her little finger. The lantern light reflected the tears in her eyes.

As scared as she was, Dixon couldn't stay angry with her. She locked her pinkie around Elizabeth's in that childhood gesture of ultimate promise.

Elizabeth's arms slid around her. Dixon became engulfed in Elizabeth's rich, warm smell and the feel of her body. Dixon's hands drifted down Elizabeth's slender back as her lips brushed her cheek.

Elizabeth's hands closed gently over Dixon's to stop them.

Realizing what she had done, Dixon yanked her hands away and stepped back. Elizabeth cupped Dixon's face. Cool, green eyes gazed up at her. Dixon tried to turn away to avoid the scrutiny, but Elizabeth's grasp was firm.

"I'm sorry," Dixon mumbled.

"I thought we settled all of that years ago," Elizabeth said, her voice as soft as cotton.

"You settled it," Dixon snapped, ashamed of her inability to control her emotions. She saw the pain in Elizabeth's eyes.

"I don't mean to hurt you," Elizabeth whispered. "You know I love you more than I love anyone else in the world."

"Yeah. I know," Dixon sniffed, trying to control her anger and embarrassment. "Just not that way."

"Dixon, we're not right for each other. A sexual relationship would destroy our friendship. We're too different. Your idea of an adventure is jumping out of a plane while mine is visiting a museum. You like camping and scuba diving. I'd rather be spending time in the library poring over old books." She wiped a tear from Dixon's cheek. "Children are a photo opportunity for you and an integral part of my world." She gazed into Dixon's eyes. "You know it wouldn't work between us."

Dixon knew that in theory she was probably right, but her heart wasn't working on theory. "I guess we'll never know," she answered brusquely, pulling Elizabeth's hands from her face and turning away.

Dixon hadn't meant to do any of this. It was supposed to have been a relaxing hiking trip. With their demanding schedules, they didn't get to see much of each other. She was between photo shoots, and Elizabeth had managed to take a few days off. It was a chance for both of them to get away and spend some time together, and now she was ruining it.

"I'm sorry I'm hurting you." Elizabeth's voice cracked. "Maybe I should go back."

7

"No!" Dixon spun and grabbed her hands. "Don't leave." She sniffed again and wiped her eyes on her shirtsleeve.

"Dix, this isn't good for you. You're a wonderful person. If you'd just let go of this idea of us, and give yourself a chance, you could find someone who'd make you happy."

"Yeah, right," Dixon scoffed. "I've got a great record so far." She would never admit that she had been telling herself the same thing through more relationships than she wanted to count.

"You've just never met the right woman."

"And who might that be?"

Elizabeth thought for a minute. "You need a woman whose sense of adventure is as great as your own. Someone who loves life and isn't afraid to live it to the fullest. And that doesn't describe me," she added with a smirk.

"Any suggestions on where I might find this wonderful mystery woman?" Dixon asked dryly.

"No. I wish I could find her for you, because your happiness means the world to me." Elizabeth looked at her closely. "Sometimes I think you use your feelings for me as an excuse to avoid having to make a real commitment to anyone else."

Dixon looked away from her. A part of her knew that Elizabeth was telling the truth, but she wasn't comfortable having her life probed, especially her love life. To change the subject Dixon asked, "What about you? What are you looking for out of life?" She didn't expect an answer to the question she had already asked a dozen times over the years.

Elizabeth frowned and gazed into the darkness. "I'm not sure. Sometimes I feel that a large chunk of me is missing. Even during those first months in a relationship, I've never felt that in-the-clouds high that everyone always talks about when she falls in love." She sighed and tilted her head to the side. "My greatest excitements have always been in my work or from a book." She gave a small sigh and continued. "When I was a kid, Jennifer was always nagging at me to get my nose out of a book and have some fun. She could never understand that reading about the daring escapes on the Underground Railroad or the great American expansion to the West was my fun, my adventure. Maybe I was born too late." A low rumble of thunder rolled far off as she turned her gaze to Dixon, who was staring in the direction of the thunder and hoping it wouldn't rain.

"Does that make any sense to you?" Elizabeth asked.

"I think so," Dixon agreed in an effort to empathize. She knew how it felt not to be able to have something you wanted, but the book part left her kind of cold.

"Dix, I want you to be happy about the baby. You know how much it means to me."

Dixon reached for Elizabeth's hand. "I am, but I'm worried about you."

"I told you, the doctor says I'm fine." Her fingers wrapped tightly around Dixon's. "I'm scared to do this alone. You've always been so much braver than me. Nothing ever frightens you. Will you help me?"

Dixon pulled Elizabeth's small body to her and

held her close. "You know I will," she whispered, determined not to let Elizabeth down. She would never let her know how frightened she had been during those long nights at the hospital or how scared she was about this pregnancy.

CHAPTER TWO

Morning found Dixon sitting on a picnic table and watching the sun climb over the horizon. The storm had not materialized, and the day was dawning with a crisp, chilling air that promised a beautiful day, perfect weather for their day of hiking.

As she sat gazing at the panoramic view, she was struck by a flash of insight. She realized that at that very second everything in her life was perfect. It might be shot to hell in the next second, but for a brief moment, there was perfection. She took a deep breath and savored the experience as she might a fine wine.

She had been coming to the Guadalupe Mountains to hike for more than twenty years and had never grown tired of watching the miracle occurring before her.

Elizabeth's hand settled on her shoulder and gently squeezed. "How did you sleep?" she asked.

Dixon fought to regain her earlier sense of perfection, but worries began to crowd in and destroy it. They had discussed until well after midnight the baby and how it would affect their lives. She still couldn't shake the nightmare of having almost lost Elizabeth. But the baby was important to Elizabeth, and Dixon was determined to stand by her through it all.

"I slept fine, except for the fact that your snoring sounded like a sawmill at full production," Dixon teased to hide her anxiety. She stood and stretched. At five-feet-eight she towered over Elizabeth's petite five-two frame.

"I do *not* snore," Elizabeth replied with great emphasis. "I merely inhale and exhale with volume."

"I'm surprised the tent didn't collapse under all that *volume!*"

"If you want breakfast, I suggest you be nice to the person who is about to feed you," Elizabeth warned.

Dixon was a notoriously horrible cook. Her idea of food for a camping trip consisted of packaged cinnamon rolls or cookies for breakfast and canned soup or chili for all other meals. When they were camping together, Elizabeth insisted on being allowed to cook a hot meal for breakfast.

Dixon ran her hands through her short, curly hair. "You know, I may have been mistaken. The noise I heard could have been the wind rushing through the canyon. In fact, now that I consider it further, I'm sure that's what was lifting the tent off the ground every time you inhaled," she stated and grinned innocently.

Elizabeth pointed a thin, well-manicured finger up at her. "You're asking for it. Now, be butch and go get the water for coffee."

Even though camping was not among Elizabeth's favorite outdoor activities, every two or three years Dixon managed to convince her to make an excursion into the Guadalupe Mountains. There they would set up a base camp, which acted as a starting point for their day trips. On very rare occasions, she could convince Elizabeth to journey to the trails that required more than a single day to complete. Trips on the longer, remoter trails took a lot more convincing, since they were not accessible by vehicle and Elizabeth and Dixon would have to carry all of their camping supplies and equipment on their backs. Dixon had learned long ago that eating meals of freeze-dried food and sleeping in a pup tent too small to stand upright in were beyond Elizabeth's tolerance.

Today they were going to take the Frijole Trail to the Frijole Ranch, proceed north to Smith Spring, and then loop back to Manzanita Spring. From there they would return to their base camp by going back over the Frijole Trail. The entire hike was approximately eight miles, but with Elizabeth along, Dixon would take it slow and spend the entire day out.

After they ate breakfast, Dixon washed the dishes at the service sink while Elizabeth secured the campsite. Afterward, Elizabeth changed into her hiking boots, and Dixon checked their backpacks, adding an extra gallon of water to hers. They had to carry their own water since none would be available after they left the campground. Lunch would be apples and sandwiches. Dixon was checking her camera equipment when Elizabeth emerged from the tent wearing a green flannel shirt, jeans, and a large canvas hat with a drawstring.

"You look ready," Dixon said, smiling at the sight of the large hat.

Elizabeth twirled about. "Am I suitably attired for a journey into the wilderness?"

Dixon nodded as she eyed Elizabeth's well-worn hiking boots with approval. The trails they were taking today were relatively easy, but the Guadalupe Mountains rose from the arid Chihuahuan Desert and was definitely an area to respect and be cautious of.

They walked in silence. Dixon's thoughts were centered around Elizabeth's accusation that Dixon was using her to avoid making a commitment to a serious relationship. *Is it true?* she wondered. Dixon shrugged away the uncomfortable thought. She admitted to herself, with some reluctance, that she did use Elizabeth as an emotional model for her lovers, and so far no one had been able to live up to that standard.

The beauty of the trail slipped by unnoticed as Dixon tried to construct a realistic view of what her life with Elizabeth could be like. With their work schedules they would rarely see each other. As a freelance photographer she traveled a lot. Of course, for Elizabeth she would be willing to cut back and work more on local shoots.

Elizabeth stayed busy helping her students after school. The baby would change that. Elizabeth would slow down now that she was pregnant, and once the baby was born she would have to shorten her hours.

Dixon allowed herself a small moment of fantasy as she pictured the three of them cozily living together.

"Slow down," Elizabeth said, panting. "You never told me this was a forced march."

Dixon glanced at her watch and mentally calculated their progress. They had been walking for less than an hour and Elizabeth was already getting tired. Maybe they would only walk to the ranch and return. "Sorry. I forgot about your delicate condition," Dixon called back as she selected a relatively flat slab of rock and removed her backpack.

"Condition, hell," Elizabeth said as Dixon helped her remove her pack. "I'm forced to take three steps to every one of yours, Ms. Paula Bunyan."

They pulled water bottles from their packs and drank deeply. Dixon replaced hers and began to snap shots of the towering slopes around them. Knowing she would grumble over having her picture taken, Dixon turned the camera on Elizabeth.

"Will you stop? You know I hate having my picture taken."

"It's for the baby," Dixon declared. "She'll want to know about her mother's younger days, and I'll have a pictorial history to share with her." She continued snapping away, until Elizabeth gave up and began to clown for the camera.

"I'm thirty-five. My younger days have already slipped by," Elizabeth stated, pulling her hat off and fluffing her hair. The temperature had grown hotter, and her sweat-dampened hair was stuck to her head. "What if the baby's a boy?" she asked, arching her eyebrows.

"Not possible," Dixon said adamantly.

"Anything's possible," Elizabeth reminded her as she tossed her hat on top of her backpack.

"Nope. I won't even consider it. It'll be a beautiful, green-eyed girl who has your looks and my charming personality," Dixon insisted, sitting back down on the rock and studying the looming limestone formations around them.

"God spare us," Elizabeth groaned before stretching out on the rock beside Dixon and closing her eyes.

"What's that up there?" Dixon asked, pointing to the slope behind them.

"A rock," Elizabeth replied sarcastically without opening her eyes.

"It looks like a cave." Dixon stood to get a better view. "I've never noticed a cave on this stretch before." She had hiked all of the trails numerous times. "Let's go look," she said eagerly.

Elizabeth opened her eyes and sat up on her elbows. "I may allow you to drag me across Texas and over mountains, but I'm not about to crawl into a cave!"

"Come on. We won't go in. We'll just look. The climb's not very steep."

"Can't you look at it from here?"

"No." Dixon was already scrambling toward it.

"Wait," Elizabeth yelled and scurried off the rock.

16

"Don't you go off and leave me out here." She practically stomped her foot as she called after Dixon in exasperation. "What about our packs?"

"Leave them. We'll only be up there a few minutes. Come on."

With a groan and a considerable amount of grumbling, Elizabeth climbed after her.

Dixon had to bend over to see into the narrow opening. "Look," she called to Elizabeth, who had caught up with her. "It's not a cave. It's a tunnel. I can see out the other side. I'm going to take a look. Hold my camera."

Elizabeth grabbed her arm. "Didn't you tell me we should never leave the trail?"

"I'm not really leaving the trail. We can still see it from here," Dixon reasoned. "I'm just going to crawl through and see what it looks like on the other side." She eased the clutching hand from her arm, but Elizabeth didn't look convinced.

"Dixon, I don't think it's a good idea," Elizabeth argued, looking suspiciously at the towering mountain above them.

Following her gaze, Dixon sighed. "This mountain has been standing here for millions of years. I seriously doubt that today is the day it's going to fall." She saw the indecision in Elizabeth's eyes and laughed. "Sit here." She patted the ground in front of the opening. "You'll be able to see me. I won't get out of your sight."

Elizabeth sat and peered into the hole. The tunnel was only about fifty feet long, and blue sky was clearly visible at the other end.

"See. It's not so bad," Dixon assured her.

"You be careful. It looks too narrow," Elizabeth

admonished Dixon as she crawled into the low opening.

Dixon was cautious where she placed her hands. She didn't need to disturb a sleeping rattlesnake or put her hand on a scorpion.

The tunnel was cold and cramped. Small outcroppings of rock tugged at her clothes and brushed against her shoulders as she eased her way through. Although not claustrophobic, Dixon felt a small tightening in her chest as she inched forward, ever vigilant of where she was. A ripple of relief ran through her as she scrambled out into the warm sunlight. She was on a slope very similar to the one at the entrance. Blaming her earlier trepidation on Elizabeth's pessimism, she brushed the dust from her knees and walked toward the edge of the slope. Her breath caught when the majestic valley below came into view. She heard Elizabeth calling, but was too caught up by the view to answer. The valley was dotted with clumps of velvet-leaf ash, bigtooth maple, and madrone. A small stream cut through one corner of the valley and disappeared between two mountains. Dixon stared in amazement. Water was a rare occurrence in this area. She was turning to go back for her camera when Elizabeth scrambled out of the tunnel with Dixon's camera around her neck.

"Damn you, Dixon. I told you not to disappear on me."

Elizabeth's breath caught as she saw the view below her. "It's beautiful," she whispered in awe.

Dixon took the camera from her and began to snap. "I never knew this was here," she breathed, unable to take her eyes from the valley. The camera emitted a low whine as it began to automatically rewind the exposed film. Dixon pulled a fresh canister from her pocket and quickly loaded it, slipping the used one into her pocket. "Maybe no one knows it's here. We may have discovered a lost valley, one in which mankind has never walked," she exclaimed, snapping away.

"I doubt if the road down there was made by Mother Nature," Elizabeth said, pointing to a faint but definite unsurfaced roadway.

"Party pooper," Dixon growled, studying the road. "It must be a service road for the park."

As they stood staring out at the vista, a faint noise reached their ears. They turned and saw a large cloud of dust working its way down the road toward them.

"Speaking of rangers, that must be one coming now," Elizabeth said, pointing. They continued to watch as the dust cloud grew nearer.

Dixon's attention was drawn to the sound, not of a vehicle's engine, but that of horses' hooves. "It sounds like horses," she said, straining to see through the dust.

They watched as a stagecoach, pursued by four horsemen, emerged from the cloud.

"What the —" Elizabeth started. "What's a stage-coach doing out here?"

"I don't know," Dixon said puzzled, automatically snapping a picture before the stagecoach disappeared around the mountain. "The park must be doing something new. There's an old stage stop not far from the ranger station. I guess it has something to do with that," she reasoned. Recalling the four horsemen, she added, "They must have been reenacting a robbery, but I don't know why they would have it way out here."

Elizabeth shrugged before commenting. "The Pinery was a stage station for the Butterfield Overland Mail. It was in operation for eleven months."

Dixon knew Elizabeth was about to launch into a history lesson. Sometimes her extensive knowledge of Texas history could be boring. Dixon tried to divert it.

"I guess with the recent funding cuts, the park has to raise revenue any way it can."

Elizabeth shook her head. "The coach was traveling too fast. It didn't look safe to me."

Dixon gave a snort of disgust. "Elizabeth, nothing is ever safe to you. Come on. Let's go get our packs." They had started toward the tunnel when they heard what sounded like firecrackers. "I guess the bad guys caught up," Dixon said with a laugh. "We'd better hurry before they come back for us."

"What?" Elizabeth scoffed, obviously stung by Dixon's earlier snide remark. "You don't want to go over there and single-handedly whip them?"

"It could make a heck of a layout for a travel magazine," Dixon said, staring toward the spot where the stage had disappeared.

Elizabeth was shaking her head and backing toward the tunnel. "No."

"It's not far," Dixon pleaded. "It has to be a new attraction. I'd be able to get some great shots."

"I'm not walking all over these mountains while you take pictures."

Dixon smiled. "We've barely got started on this trail. I'll make a deal with you. You go with me to the stage station so I can take a few shots and we'll go back to camp as soon as I'm finished." *We'll practically be back at the camp anyway,* Dixon thought.

It was little more than a quarter mile from the ranger station to their campsite.

Elizabeth eyed her suspiciously before asking, "We won't have to finish this trail?"

"No. You can spend the rest of the day lying in your hammock, reading."

Elizabeth hesitated. "What about our packs?"

Dixon knew she had her. "I'll come back later and pick them up. No one will bother them."

"All right," Elizabeth relented, "but you'd better not be tricking me."

"Pinkie swear," Dixon said, extending her little finger.

CHAPTER THREE

The terrain was a gradual downhill slope and easy walking, but it still took them a half hour to reach the stage station. Dixon stopped sharply. The last time she had seen the station two or three years ago it had been a pile of rubble. Now a tall, limestone wall met them. Dixon and Elizabeth made their way to where the huge wooden gate stood open. The limestone wall formed a tight rectangle. A cabin sat at the back, a short distance from them. The stagecoach was in front of it with its doors thrown open. The lathered horses stood with their heads hanging in exhaustion. Dixon could see what looked like four bodies scattered around it.

"Talk about realism," Elizabeth said softly. "They ran those poor horses almost to death."

Elizabeth was right, Dixon admitted to herself. The horses had been pushed too hard.

They stood for several seconds staring at the scene. Dixon tried to ignore the prickling sensation that crept up her neck.

"Dixon, I don't like this. Let's go back." Elizabeth's voice held that soft, hesitant sound that grated on Dixon.

Something told her to follow Elizabeth's advice, but her incurable curiosity drove her on. "They're just dummies. Come on. Everyone's probably inside bellying up to the bar." She forced a smile and took Elizabeth's hand, pulling her along.

Afterward, Dixon could never say for sure when they determined that the bodies lying before them were human and not cotton-stuffed dummies. She remembered hearing Elizabeth's gasp and watching her run to the first body. The man was dressed in what Dixon assumed was authentic Western garb, but there was no doubt that the sinister black hole in his forehead was genuine. Dixon felt the bile rise into her throat as she stared at the blood-soaked ground beneath his head. She had never seen a dead person except at funerals, and they were all in considerably better shape than was the man before her.

Elizabeth had moved from body to body and was yelling for her. "Help me here, Dixon!"

The sound of Elizabeth's voice became a lifeline for

Dixon, and she stumbled toward it. Elizabeth was leaning over a woman, who was dressed in a blue hoopskirt. The bodice was covered in blood.

"She's still alive," Elizabeth said. "Carry her inside."

Dixon gathered the woman in her arms and stumbled toward the cabin. With lifeless eyes staring up at her, a man lay sprawled halfway out the open door. Dixon averted her gaze and stepped over him. She eased the woman onto the long table, which sat directly in front of a large fireplace. "I'll check the rest," she said and started for the door.

"I already have. They're dead." Elizabeth ripped the woman's bodice open. "Find me some clean towels and see if there's any hot water."

Dixon turned to begin her search, but Elizabeth's voice stopped her.

"First, maybe you should get his guns," she prompted, and nodded at the dead man in the doorway. "And then go close the gate. We don't know where those men went."

Dixon's heart skipped a beat. She had forgot about the four horsemen. She ran to close the gate and drop the bar in place. As she started back to the house, she was struck by a moment of sheer terror when she realized the men could still be somewhere in the compound and she had latched the gate, locking them all in together. She glanced around wildly. If they were here, where could they be?

The only structures were the cabin, a shed that was attached to an open corral, and a small building off to the far end of the rectangle. The smaller building was too tiny for four men to fit into, but it could easily hold one. Dixon eased her way toward it, trying desperately to decide what she would do if someone waited inside. Common sense told her the men were long gone, but the burning fear in her chest wouldn't rest until she checked. She was within six feet of the building when her nostrils picked up the stench. She didn't need one of Elizabeth's history lessons to know the building was an outhouse. Unable to walk away without checking, she threw open the door. Nothing but the loud drone of flies greeted her. Holding her nose and fighting the roll of her stomach, she raced to the shed.

As she approached, Dixon saw that the large wooden latch was slipped securely in place. It was probably impossible for anyone to hide inside and pull the latch across after them, but again she felt compelled to check. Dixon stood outside the door of the shed. Why had she insisted on crawling through that stupid tunnel? None of this would have happened if they had stuck to their original plans. *Like Elizabeth wanted*, a small voice nagged.

Her heart hammered against her chest as she lifted the latch and threw the door open. She was greeted by the smell of fresh hay and dust, which produced a vigorous sneeze from her. She peered in cautiously before stepping into the shed. As her eyes adjusted to the dim interior, she was able to identify several burlap bags of what she suspected was feed for the horses. Two large wooden bins were along the side wall. She peeked into the one nearest her, half expecting a towering, gun-toting bulk to jump out at her. All that greeted her was the rich smell of oats.

"I'm getting as jumpy as Elizabeth," she muttered. She spied a wooden ladder that led to the loft. It could easily hold four men. She placed a hand on the frame and was startled when her camera bumped against one of the rungs. She looked down at it, surprised to find it still hung around her neck. The cool, familiar shape of the camera in her hand gave her a feeling of calmness. Taking a deep breath she climbed slowly upward, telling herself she was being silly. The men obviously would not have hidden themselves in here. The sweet smell of hay grew stronger. *The killers left before we arrived,* she continued to reassure herself. She inched her way upward until she reached the loft. It was filled with nothing more sinister than hay.

Dixon gave a nervous, self-conscious laugh. If Elizabeth could see her now, she wouldn't think she was so brave. She ran her hands through her hair before letting them drop sharply against her thighs. There was a sudden noise behind her. She whirled to confront her attacker as something struck sharply against the side of her face. Dixon launched herself backward and felt her heel slip over the ledge of the loft. She grabbed out frantically and caught nothing but air. Her stomach gave a sickening lurch as she fell. She landed on the row of feedbags with no more damage than her breath being momentarily knocked from her and her pride being dented. She wouldn't tell Elizabeth how an owl had frightened her so badly she had fallen from the hayloft. She brushed herself off and ran back to the cabin.

She stopped at the doorway, staring at the dead man and the guns Elizabeth earlier had instructed her to take. She knew she couldn't touch him.

"Dixon. Dixon!" Elizabeth's voice cut through her fear. She looked up to find Elizabeth's cool green eyes watching her. She felt mesmerized by their intensity. "You've always been the bravest person I've ever known. Don't change now."

Dixon swallowed sharply, snatched the rifle from his hands, and pulled the pistol from his belt. There was no way she could make herself unbuckle the pistol belt. Using her foot, she rolled him outside as gently as possible and slammed the heavy door. She saw a thick length of wood leaning next to her against the wall. She placed the weapons on the floor and picked up the brace. Its weight felt reassuring as she slid it into the slots on either side of the door. She patted the door with approval. It would take more than four men to break in that baby.

"Here," she said, retrieving the weapons and laying them across the end of the table.

Elizabeth was pressing a torn piece of the woman's dress against both sides of her shoulder.

"I need those towels, Dixon. I can't get the bleeding to stop."

The room whirled crazily when Dixon saw the massive amount of blood that stained the woman's front and Elizabeth's hands. Glad to have something to do somewhere else, she rushed off to hunt for clean towels.

There were no signs of any modern conveniences. The house was divided into three rooms. The long room where Elizabeth worked on the wounded woman ran the width of the building. Two smaller ones sat behind it. In the first one, Dixon found a bed and a table that held a porcelain washbowl and pitcher. A man's faded blue shirt and a pair of pants lay over the back of a wooden chair. The second smaller room seemed to be a storage area. Several barrels were lined against one wall. A metal can marked KEROSENE stood alone in one corner.

Dixon grunted in disgust as she turned and found large slabs of meat hanging from the rafters. Not seeing anything she could use, she hurried back to Elizabeth.

In addition to the long table, the main room held several straight-backed wooden chairs and numerous black-bottomed pots that were suspended from hooks over the fireplace. Despite the heat of the day, a low fire burned. For the first time, Dixon became aware of the smell of beans cooking. She noticed the large pot hanging over the fire. There was also a heavy-looking cast-iron kettle sitting on the floor of the fireplace near the low flame.

A wooden bar, like the ones she had seen in saloons on television westerns, ran across the end of the room. Judging from the look of the furniture, the place had been restored with replicas of its original furnishings.

Dixon found several clean rags on one of the shelves beneath the bar and gave them to Elizabeth, who was still clamping the bloody scraps of material from the woman's dress over the wound.

"I'll need your help," Elizabeth directed. "Tear some of those rags into strips and make two thick pads." Dazed, Dixon complied.

"Now tear two long strips to use as ties."

Dixon tore the strips and followed Elizabeth's instructions as they wrapped a tight bandage over the gaping wound in the woman's shoulder. Dixon's stomach turned at the sight of the mess.

As Elizabeth tied the last knot she nodded to Dixon. "You can let go now."

Dixon stood staring at her hands, transfixed by the blood that stained them.

"Why don't you go wash up, while I finish here?" Elizabeth urged.

"There's a washbasin in the bedroom," Dixon mumbled.

"Bring back a blanket if you can find one," Elizabeth instructed. "We don't want her to go into shock."

"There's probably something in the bedroom," Dixon said. "I'll be right back." She stumbled to the bedroom, afraid she was going to be sick. The porcelain pitcher was full of water, and Dixon frantically scrubbed the sticky blood off her hands.

When Dixon returned with a somewhat musty blanket from the bedroom, Elizabeth was gently washing away the drying blood that had run across the woman's neck and chest.

"Where did you find water?" Dixon asked numbly.

Elizabeth nodded toward the kettle at the fireplace. She looked up to find Dixon's pale face watching her. "You should probably keep watch at the window to make sure no one sneaks up on us. I doubt if that wall would stop anyone who was determined to get in."

Relieved to get away from the sight of so much blood, Dixon stood at the filmy window and stared out. She could see two of the dead men lying in the dirt, and she averted her gaze. To the left front of the house, and attached to the shed that had been the scene of Dixon's earlier humiliation, was a corral.

Several horses milled inside. Had the men swapped their tired mounts for fresh ones from the horses kept for pulling the stage? They probably had a getaway car waiting for them at one of the park entrances. It would be a simple enough matter to ride the horses until they neared one of the trails and then to walk out of the park like any other hiker. She studied the yard and the stagecoach, careful to avoid looking at the bodies.

"Why would anyone do this?" she asked, and continued without waiting for an answer. "What did the stage carry that could be worth shooting four people for?"

"People kill for all sorts of reasons. Who knows why?" Elizabeth sounded preoccupied.

"Do you think they were park personnel, or visitors?" Dixon asked, her gaze settling on the man lying by the stagecoach. The sight of blood caused her to slam her eyes shut. She rushed on, desperate to hear the sound of her own voice, to know that with so much death so near, she still lived. She didn't want to contemplate what would have happened had she and Elizabeth arrived a few minutes earlier. Or how different it would have been if Elizabeth hadn't been along, her shorter strides slowing them down. Alone, it would have taken Dixon only half the time to get to the station from the slope.

"They must be park personnel since they're in costume." Dixon shivered and continued. "I doubt visitors would go to all the trouble of getting dressed up like that just to ride on a stage." She knew she was rambling but couldn't stop. "There're so few visitors here during this time of year. Why would they even be running the stage? Why would they run it at any time? The park is more suited for serious hikers and backpackers. There's not much here to attract the regular RV and camping crowds." Dixon stopped to catch her breath, but the silence closed around her. "Do you realize we haven't seen another hiker all day?" she asked, stunned by the thought. The park was by no means crowded, but it was unusual not to have seen someone.

"Are you okay?" Elizabeth's touch startled her. "You're rambling."

"Yeah." Dixon clutched her hand. "I'm just trying to figure out what the hell happened."

"I don't know, but we've got to get help. She's lost a lot of blood," Elizabeth said and glanced back at the woman on the table.

"How do we get her out of here? We could go as far as the tunnel on horseback, but what then?" Dixon asked. Neither seemed to have an answer, so they stood observing the peaceful movement of the horses in the corral.

Dixon watched as Elizabeth moved from the window to the table and gazed down at the woman. "I don't think we should attempt to move her. You'll have to go for help."

"I'm not leaving you alone," Dixon protested.

"Dixon, we don't have a choice. She could die without medical attention. The bullet went through her shoulder, so that's not a problem, but she has lost a lot of blood and needs to be in a hospital."

Dixon stared at the woman and saw what she hadn't noticed before. The woman was beautiful in a pale, delicate type of way. She had long, dark lashes, a thin, aristocratic nose, and full lips. Her dark hair, which had been caught up by a wide, ivory clip, was coming loose and cascading around her head on the table. Dixon guessed her to be in her late twenties.

"Dixon, you have to go."

"No. I'm not going to leave you. What if they come back?" A fog seemed to lift from Dixon's mind. Why hadn't she thought of it sooner? She grabbed Elizabeth's arm. "We're practically at the ranger station. We're so close they should have heard the shots. They'll come to investigate."

Elizabeth shook her head without taking her gaze from the woman. "We can't be sure of that. You're always telling me how sound and sights are distorted here because of the mountains," Elizabeth reminded her. She brushed the hair away from the unconscious woman's forehead.

The act was so tender and intimate that Dixon was forced to look away.

Elizabeth continued as she pulled the blanket higher up on the woman's shoulder. "As fast as you walk, you can get to the ranger station quickly and have them call for medical help." Elizabeth took her hands. "You have to be careful. Those men may still be nearby."

"Which is precisely why I'm not leaving you," Dixon argued.

"All right," Elizabeth sighed. "I'll go."

"Bull!" Dixon stepped in front of the door.

"Get out of my way."

"Liz, you've said yourself we don't know where those men are. You're not leaving alone. There are four of them. At least if we stay together we have a chance if they come back. The rangers will find us."

A look of determination, the likes of which Dixon

had never seen before, settled over Elizabeth's face. A small shiver coursed down Dixon's spine.

"Move, Dixon."

"And if I don't?" Dixon's voice sounded thin and uncertain. For a brief flash she wondered if she was afraid of Elizabeth. The thought of her own towering bulk being frightened by the tiny woman before her should have amused her, but there was nothing amusing in the look Elizabeth gave her.

After a long moment of silence, Dixon gave in. "I'll go." She was relieved to see Elizabeth's eyes soften.

"Thank you," she said, gripping Dixon's hands. "Take one of the guns and hurry."

"I'll be back as soon as I can," Dixon promised. She removed the camera that still hung around her neck and picked up the pistol. She held it away from her. "I have no earthly idea what to do with this thing," she admitted, staring at it with distaste.

Elizabeth took the weapon from her and released a pin. "This is the cylinder," she explained as she popped the circular mechanism out. "The pistol hasn't been fired, so you still have six rounds." She secured the cylinder as Dixon looked on dumbfounded. "To fire it, simply pull back the hammer, point it as you would point your finger, and squeeze the trigger. Squeeze it. Don't jerk it."

"How do you know so much about guns?" Dixon asked as Elizabeth handed the pistol back to her.

"I have no idea," Elizabeth admitted. "Until now I've never touched a gun."

"Then how . . . ?" Dixon was about to pursue the matter, but Elizabeth was pushing her toward the door. "Hurry," she urged.

Dixon left the station at a run. She kept glancing at the mountains around her, imagining a madman with a gun watching her from every shadow. The pistol she clutched in her hand did nothing to alleviate her fears. If anything, it only added to them. It was a constant reminder of what she had left behind. The knowledge of what would happen to Elizabeth if the men should return made her run harder.

Her breathing grew labored, and sweat poured into her eyes, blinding her. The heavy hiking boots felt like lead weights pulling at her feet. Her side flared with pain that intensified until she was forced to slow her pace to a fast walk. She looked behind her. The stage station was no longer in sight. She followed the rough path that had been worn by numerous trips of the stagecoach. The deeply rutted and uneven ground made running difficult. When the pain in her side eased, she began to run again.

Dixon's lungs felt as if they would explode. Her calves were on fire with pain and knotted with cramps as she struggled to the top of the rise. *The ranger station should be in a valley just over this ridge*, she thought. She called up her last reserve of strength and burst over the top. Her strangled cry for help froze in her throat as she gazed at the empty valley before her. She glanced around wildly. The ranger station had to be here. She knew this area like the back of her hand. She forced down the panic that seeped in. She had left the stage station with no water, and now she was lost.

Dixon made herself take several deep breaths before she surveyed her surroundings. She obviously hadn't gone as far as she had thought, she told herself. Standing atop the ridge, she scanned the horizon for landmarks. In the distance almost directly in front of her loomed Guadalupe Peak, to the left was the undeniable outline of El Capitan. The faint trail of the stage route crawled across the valley and disappeared. Every fiber of her being told her that the ranger station should be in the valley directly below her. She collapsed on a large rock and forced herself to draw a mental map of the area she had covered today.

Judging from where the stage route disappeared, it was obvious it didn't begin at the ranger station as they had assumed, but that didn't explain why the station wasn't in the valley below her. She studied the rising slopes to her right and suddenly remembered crawling through the tunnel. She jumped up, excited. She wasn't lost. She was simply looking at a similar valley that was close enough to the station to share similar landmarks. That explained why the area below her just looked familiar. There had to be thousands of tiny valleys like this one scattered throughout the mountains. All she had to do was go back through the tunnel and return to the station from there.

She would have to return to the stage station first, and then go back through the tunnel. Exhausted but relieved, she headed back at a steady trot.

Dixon drank deeply from the cup of water Elizabeth handed her. Elizabeth, holding the rifle, had met her at the gate. Dixon again avoided looking at the dead bodies as she and Elizabeth made their way into the house.

"What happened?" Elizabeth asked after Dixon had finished gulping another cup of the water.

"When we crawled through the tunnel, it put us on the other side of the slope from the ranger station, and I lost my bearing. I'll have to go back the way we came." Dixon glanced at the woman who lay on the table. "How is she?"

"She's still unconscious, but the bleeding has stopped. I guess all we have to worry about now is her going into shock. I wish I knew more about treating wounds."

Dixon squeezed her arm. "Let me find something to carry water in, and I'll take off."

"You rest," Elizabeth said, pushing her into one of the chairs. "I saw a canteen earlier. I'll fill it for you."

A short time later, Dixon once more hurried out of the wooden gate, this time without the heavy pistol. She had decided she had a greater chance of shooting herself than she had of shooting the killers.

She had no problem retracing their route to the slope where they had earlier exited the tunnel. Once she was on the other side, it would take her less than thirty minutes to reach the ranger station.

She raced up the slope to the tunnel and was met by a solid wall. Puzzled, she looked around. The same view that she and Elizabeth had enjoyed such a short time ago was there, but she couldn't find the opening. She ran up and down the slope several times trying to find a different pathway, but nothing led her back to the tunnel. Desperate, she tried to find a way over the mountain, but it was too steep. After nearly two hours, she gave up and stumbled back to the stage stop.

Elizabeth met her at the door of the cabin. The

valley was already growing dark, and a night chill was settling in. The horses still stood hitched to the stage, but the bodies were no longer lying in the yard or on the porch.

"I put them in the shed," Elizabeth said to Dixon's observations. "What happened?"

"I couldn't find the tunnel." Dixon was ashamed of having failed twice.

"Come on in. I found some coffee, and that pot of beans is ready." Elizabeth's voice held an eerie calmness.

"How is she?" Dixon asked, staring at the woman.

"If I can keep the wound from getting infected, I think she'll be all right." She poured coffee into a metal cup. "I found a pump around back. Get washed up, and I'll have this ready by the time you get back. To work the pump you just — " She made a pumping motion with her arm.

"Yeah, I know what you're talking about," Dixon replied. She found the pump and soon worked out a system of pumping with one hand and rubbing the water over her sweat-stained body with the other. She was soaked and freezing by the time she returned to the doorway.

Elizabeth grinned and tossed her a thin, rough towel. "You look like a drowned kitten. I didn't mean for you to take a shower under the pump."

"I didn't intend to," Dixon admitted, her teeth chattering slightly. "The water felt so good I couldn't stop." The mountains turned cold at night. It was hard to remember that just a few hours ago the temperature had been soaring into the high eighties. She rubbed herself dry with the towel.

Elizabeth had placed the coffee and a plate of

beans on the table near the fire. Several large chunks of bread sat on a plate in the middle of the table. The aroma of the beans reminded Dixon that she was starved. She hadn't eaten since breakfast. Neither of them spoke until Dixon pushed away her plate and sat enjoying the coffee.

For a few minutes, Dixon had forgotten why they were at this place. The beans settled like a lead plate when she thought about the dead men who lay in the cold shed. "Someone should be here soon to check on the stage," Dixon said, sipping the hot brew. She didn't want to spend the night here.

"Maybe," Elizabeth replied.

"When they don't show up home or report back to wherever the stage originated, someone will investigate." Dixon realized her voice had grown shrill with fear.

Elizabeth patted her hand. "I think we should plan on standing guard all night. Why don't you get some sleep? I'll wake you when I get sleepy."

"Someone will be here shortly," Dixon persisted.

"We should be prepared anyway. Just in case no one misses them tonight," Elizabeth insisted. She stood and walked to the window to look out. "Before you go to bed, do you think you could get the horses unhitched and into the corral?"

Dixon sighed. She had worked at a horse stable for a summer, but unhitching horses from a stagecoach hadn't been part of the job duties. Still, it was probably just a combination of buckled harnesses, she thought wearily.

"Let me see if I can figure it out," she said and struggled to her feet.

Elizabeth lit an oil lamp for Dixon to use and began to clear away the dishes.

It took Dixon several minutes to figure out how to remove the harnesses from the animals. She led them into the corral and was met by a chorus of hungry snorts from the horses already there. She would have to feed them.

It took her several minutes to work up the courage to enter the shed, where the dead men lay, to get hay and a large bucket of oats to feed all of the horses. She pumped buckets of fresh water to pour into the large watering trough that sat in the corner of the corral.

When she returned an hour later, Dixon gave in to Elizabeth's suggestion to sleep. She didn't want to admit that she was totally exhausted.

Dixon stood by the basin in the small bedroom and stared into the tarnished square of mirror that hung over it. The flicker of the oil lamp on the small table beside her made her reflection appear to be moving. Her eyes seemed larger and darker, and her skin paler and thinner. Too many thoughts raced through her head. She shook it, trying to clear them away.

She longed to be back in her comfortable apartment, with her fish tank and her sweet but somewhat nosy neighbor, Mrs. Jenkins.

She rubbed her hands over her face. The night was so silent. Nothing could be heard scurrying around in the darkness. For some reason she found the silence chilling. "You just need a good night's sleep," she admonished herself. Tomorrow someone would come to rescue them.

She stretched her tired body across the squeaky bed that smelled of an unknown person, probably one of the dead men. She tried to sleep, but she couldn't keep her mind off of Elizabeth being alone in the other room. Or at least, that's what she kept telling herself as she stripped the quilts and blanket off the bed and grabbed a pillow.

Elizabeth sat staring at the sleeping woman as Dixon spread the quilts in front of the fireplace and soon fell fast asleep.

Dixon woke to the sound of birds chirping. For a brief moment she prepared herself to go sit on her favorite picnic table and watch the sun break the horizon. As the fog of sleep cleared from her mind, the events of yesterday rushed over her. She sat up with a start. The front door was open, and there was no sign of Elizabeth.

Dixon fought her way out of the tangle of quilts and grabbed the pistol from the table where she had laid it the night before. As she rushed out the door she found Elizabeth standing in the gateway watching the sunrise. Elizabeth turned and smiled at her.

Dixon felt her breath catch. She had never seen such serenity as was reflected in Elizabeth's face. *It must be the baby*, Dixon grudgingly admitted to herself.

Elizabeth extended her hand to her. As Dixon took it, Elizabeth turned back to the morning spectacle.

"Why didn't you wake me?"

"I never got sleepy. Rachel woke shortly after you went to sleep, and we talked for a while."

"Rachel?" Dixon's memory faltered a moment before she realized they must be talking about the wounded woman. She spun to stare back into the cabin. The woman was no longer on the table. "Where is she?" Dixon demanded, fearing the worst.

"She was feeling better, so I helped her to the bed. The table had got uncomfortable for her. She's still sleeping."

"You should've waked me. I would've helped you. Elizabeth, you should try to rest," Dixon insisted and studied her friend with concern.

"I'm fine."

"You've got to think of the baby now." Even as she argued with her, Dixon had to admit she had never seen Elizabeth looking better. She positively glowed.

Elizabeth turned to her, and again Dixon was jolted by the look of completeness.

"I've never felt better in my life. I've finally found what I've been looking for. Thanks to you my dear, dear friend." She suddenly hugged Dixon so tightly she winced.

"Liz, you're scaring me. What's going on?" No one but Dixon was allowed to use the shortened version of Elizabeth's name, and even she rarely got away with it.

Elizabeth pulled away and tiptoed to kiss Dixon's cheek. "Let me get some coffee started first. I know you can't function without it. Why don't you bring in a few big armloads of that wood over there for me?" She pointed to a large pile stacked against the side of the shed.

"Liz?" For some unexplainable reason, Dixon felt a

ripple of fear, and it had nothing to do with the dead this time.

Elizabeth pushed her toward the woodpile before Dixon could continue. "Coffee first," she said smiling serenely.

Dixon continued to carry wood until the large box by the fireplace was full. The vague sense of dread grew stronger and pushed her to stay busy. When the wood box was full, she went to the corral and saw to the horses. She was careful to avoid looking around when she entered the shed for hay and oats.

Dixon entered the house to the smell of coffee and bacon. Elizabeth tucked some papers into her hip pocket as Dixon came in.

"I fed the horses. I guess that summer job working at the horse stables in Brackenridge Park finally paid off," Dixon stated.

"I don't know anything about horses. Maybe next time you could show me how to feed them, so I'll be able to help you."

Dixon stared at her. "I'm going for help today. I was probably in shock yesterday, and that's why I couldn't find the tunnel."

Elizabeth turned back to the fireplace. "Sit down," she said, motioning for Dixon to sit at the table as she took the coffeepot from the hearth. Elizabeth carefully poured two cups before setting the pot on the hearth near the flames. "Drink your coffee. I'll have breakfast ready in a couple of minutes."

Dixon again noticed the papers in Elizabeth's hip pocket. She thought she recognized one of them as being the park's literature on the stage stop. "Is that the brochure on the stage stop you have in your pocket?" she asked.

Elizabeth became very still and seemed reluctant to answer her. "Yes," she admitted. "I picked it up when we were registering, and I brought it with me yesterday to read."

"Can I see it? Maybe it gives a schedule of when the stagecoach rides occur. Then we'll know when to expect someone."

"There's no schedule. I've already checked," Elizabeth stated. She removed the brochure from her pocket but continued to hold it.

"There's bound to be something," Dixon argued. She was beginning to get that prickly feeling along her neck again. She wished someone would hurry up and get there to rescue them.

Elizabeth slid the brochure back into her pocket and removed the skillet of bacon from the fire. She quickly divided the bacon onto two plates. After placing the skillet on the hearth, she brought over a large loaf of bread from a cover on the bar and sliced off two chunks. "Eat," she commanded, placing a plate in front of Dixon. She layered several slices of bacon over her own bread, folded it, and began to eat.

"I don't see how you can calmly sit there eating when we may be out here with a group of madmen."

Elizabeth looked at her closely. "Dixon, you have my word that we've never been safer."

Dixon started to protest, but Elizabeth held up her hand. There was that look of determination in her eyes again that made Dixon hesitate. She began to eat.

They ate in silence. Dixon fought the rising fear that kept plucking at her. When they finished eating, Elizabeth poured Dixon more coffee before sitting down across from her.

"Dixon, I'm going to tell you something and you're

not going to believe me, but you have to promise me you'll hear me out. Will you do that?"

Dixon's heart was pounding overtime, and despite the chilly morning temperature, sweat was breaking out on her back. Some inner warning system was telling her to run, but Elizabeth's cool, green eyes kept her rooted in place. Unable to speak, Dixon nodded.

Elizabeth took Dixon's hands inside her smaller ones. Dixon found herself staring at the hands that she had always considered frail but which now conveyed a sense of strength.

"Something happened yesterday when we crawled through the tunnel. I'm not going to try to explain it or pretend I even know how it happened, but we're no longer where we were when we left camp yesterday morning."

"Of course not." Dixon couldn't believe the thick, coarse voice she heard was actually her own. She tried to swallow, but her mouth was bone dry. She pulled one hand free and gulped the burning coffee, barely noticing its scalding effect on her mouth. "We're on the other side of the mountain now. We're at the old stage stop."

Elizabeth squeezed the hand she still held. "We're at the stage stop all right, but it isn't old. In fact," she added softly, "it's almost brand-new."

"It's been restored," Dixon snapped, no longer caring if Elizabeth saw her fear.

"No, sugar, it's brand-new. Dixon, somehow we've stepped back in time."

"Bullshit!" Dixon pushed away from the table so violently that her chair overturned and her coffee splashed over the table.

Elizabeth patiently mopped up the spilled coffee with a rag and removed the brochure from her pocket. "I think you should read this," she said, pushing the paper across the table.

Dixon stared at the paper as though it were a twelve-foot rattlesnake. As long as she didn't touch it, her life would remain sane. She turned her gaze to Elizabeth and struggled for a logical conclusion. "It's the altitude," she challenged. "You're hallucinating or something. You haven't slept and you're completely exhausted. I'll go get help." Dixon grabbed the canteen and filled it with water from a wooden bucket that sat on the bar before she started toward the door.

"Dixon, I don't think the tunnel is there anymore."

Dixon ignored her as she ran from the house. She continued to run until her sides ached and her stomach heaved so violently that she vomited her breakfast. She sat in the shade of a ledge and rested until her sides stopped hurting. Elizabeth was obviously delusional. There was a valid explanation to everything that had happened, and it certainly wasn't some kind of time warp. The stage station had been renovated and the victims were park personnel dressed in period clothing. The world was full of psychos who killed for no reason. There *was* a reasonable explanation for this mess.

She found the slope easily, but again there was no sign of the tunnel. She walked several miles beyond the point where the tunnel had been. Common sense told her she was an experienced enough hiker to know where they had been yesterday, but Elizabeth's suspicions drove her on. *There's no such thing as a time warp.* She repeated the line until it became a mantra. No matter how hard she fought them, fragments of articles and discussions intruded to haunt her. Hadn't Einstein had a theory about time travel? She pushed it away, but it kept returning. What was the Philadelphia Experiment? Didn't it have something to do with travel between different time dimensions? Or was it just a movie? She continued to search until the sun dipped below the horizon. Exhausted and scared, she made her way back to the stage station.

A warm glow greeted her from the window of the cabin. She stood for several minutes and ignored the chilly evening air settling around her. She watched as Elizabeth moved around preparing supper. Did she actually love her, or was Elizabeth so attractive because she was unattainable? Confused, Dixon turned away and went to the corral to check on the horses again but was shocked to see they were gone. Returning from the corral, she realized the stage was no longer sitting in front of the cabin. Someone had come to rescue them. She rushed inside.

"What happened to the stage and the horses?" she shouted as she burst through the door, looking for whoever was there to rescue them.

"It's a long story. I'll tell you after supper. Let's just eat now and enjoy ourselves for a while."

Elizabeth's words were crisp as she set the table. They again carried that tone of finality. Dixon shivered and suddenly didn't want to know what had happened to the stage or the horses. She somehow sensed it was going to create another unwanted change.

"How's Rachel?" She forced her voice to remain calm. Everything would be all right if they just maintained a normal conversation. No more talk about time dimensions and murders. The room suddenly felt too hot and close. Dixon got up to open the door to let in fresh air.

Elizabeth placed plates on the table as she spoke. "She was awake for several hours today. I just fed her a bowl of broth, and she's sleeping again."

Dixon imagined for a moment that she saw a softening in Elizabeth's face when she spoke of Rachel.

After a meal of stew and bread, Elizabeth pulled the park brochure from her pocket and pushed it toward Dixon.

"After you read this, we need to talk. I'm going to check on Rachel. When I come back, we can discuss it." Elizabeth left the offending paper on the table in front of Dixon and gave her a light hug before leaving.

Dixon stared at the paper for some time before she pulled it to her. She moved closer to the light of the fireplace and began to read.

In 1858 the Butterfield Overland Mail line began a stage route between Missouri and California. The stage station was named for the forests of pines that were located nearby. It was in operation for eleven months until the stationmaster, a stage driver, and two passengers were killed during a daring robbery. A third passenger, Benjamin Short, was severely wounded but managed to ride thirty miles to the nearest ranch, owned by J. C. Mueller, to report the robbery. Mr. Mueller sent a ranch hand to report the incident to the county authorities, while he and two of his sons rode to the stage stop to bury the dead. Benjamin Short's wife, Rachel, was one of the passengers

killed during the robbery. The bandits were
captured a short time later. The station was
soon replaced by a less remote stop to the south
near where Interstate 10 now runs. The
crumbled remains of the Pinery are now
guarded by the four stark crosses erected on a
hill.

Dixon quickly glanced at the date of the brochure. It was only two months old. She heard Elizabeth's steps and raised her face to stare at her. "There's an explanation for this," she whispered weakly.

Elizabeth's face was filled with compassion as she reached for Dixon's hand. She walked her to the open doorway and pointed to the ridge beyond the wall. Three crudely formed crosses stood silhouetted against the moonlit sky. Dixon felt her knees grow weak.

"We've already changed history," Elizabeth said.

"It's impossible to change history. How could we change something that happened over a hundred years ago?" Dixon's anger, born of fear, was reflected in her voice.

"Because somehow we've stepped back in time," Elizabeth said quietly.

"Will you stop that bullshit!" Dixon wanted to run, to return to their base camp, to go home to her comfortable apartment — to be anywhere except here. "There's a reasonable explanation for this. We just have to find it."

"It's right there in black and white," Elizabeth said and pointed to the brochure that Dixon was clutching. "Rachel was supposed to die, but we arrived in time to save her."

"It's a misprint!" Dixon screamed. "It wasn't some

hundred-year-old rancher who buried them. You buried them while I was gone today."

Elizabeth shook her head and helped Dixon back to her chair. She took a deep breath. "After you left this morning, I hitched the horses back to the stage." She ran a hand through her hair and met Dixon's doubting eyes. "I moved the three bodies back out to about where we found them and then I sat with Rachel. I watched the men ride in and bury the dead." Her voice faltered slightly. "One of them came into the house. I could hear him moving around, and he came into the bedroom."

"Someone was here and you didn't leave!" Dixon jumped from her chair and towered over Elizabeth.

Elizabeth held up her hand to stop her. "Sit down, please." She turned her attention to the blazing fire.

Dixon obediently took her seat.

"He never saw us," Elizabeth explained.

"I thought you said he went into the bedroom. Were you hiding?"

Elizabeth's gaze again locked with hers. "No, we weren't hiding. He looked right at us as if we weren't there and then left. I think he was looking for Rachel. The brochure said she died, but I think we changed everything when we arrived and kept her from bleeding to death."

"Why didn't he see you?" Dixon insisted, ignoring her explanation. "Rachel sees you? Why can she see you and he can't?" The sarcasm dripped from Dixon's words.

"Rachel was asleep when they came, so I'm the only one who saw him, and I don't know why he couldn't see us. Maybe by somehow changing history we are no longer a part of it." Elizabeth sighed deeply

49

and shrugged. "When they left they took the stage with them."

"How did you manage to get the horses hitched back to the stage?" Dixon asked suspiciously. "I barely managed to get them unhooked, and I've had a lot more experience with horses than you."

Elizabeth shrugged. "It . . . it was like I'd been doing it all my life. I can't explain it. The same way I can't explain how I knew how to operate the Dutch oven for the biscuits tonight, and how I knew they would be coming to bury the dead today."

Dixon looked over her shoulder at the three lonely crosses on the hill. "I'm not going to be able to rationalize this away, am I?" she asked in a voice that shook.

"Not this time."

They sat quietly, each lost in her own thoughts. Dixon walked to the door. "Is it really 1859?"

She heard Elizabeth let out a long breath before she spoke.

"Rachel says they left San Francisco on April 2, 1859. They had been traveling for fourteen days when the robbery occurred."

Dixon scrubbed her hands across her face. Maybe if she rubbed hard enough she would wake up from this nightmare.

"How's she handling being rescued by a couple of pants-wearing females from the twentieth century?" Dixon gave a weak smile at the absurdity of her question. Perhaps they were both delusional.

"About like you're handling being sent back a hundred and thirty years."

"And you?" Dixon asked as she turned back to face her.

Elizabeth's gaze slid away from Dixon. She plucked at a loose string on her shirt. "I feel at peace." She answered so gently that Dixon had to lean forward to hear her. "I think this is where I was meant to be." She stood and began to pace by the table. "All my life I've felt . . . out of step with the rest of the world, as though something were missing. I've never felt complete." Dixon recalled Elizabeth having said practically the same words just the day before. "Here I feel whole."

"What do we do now?" Dixon asked, unwilling to pursue Elizabeth's admission.

"I don't know. I've read a little on the theory of concurrent time dimensions, but I'm no expert."

"Tell me what you know."

"Dixon, this whole concept is unproven theories."

"Well, those unproved theories are looking pretty accurate right now, and it's all we have to work with."

Elizabeth sighed. "According to what I've read, some researchers believe that there are windows between these different dimensions and that they open and close at intervals."

"So that's why I can't find the tunnel anymore. The window, in this case, is the tunnel that has closed," Dixon reasoned.

"Probably."

"Are there ways to make the windows reopen, or is it time controlled or what?"

"I don't know."

"Do we camp on the slope and keep watch until the tunnel reopens, or will we just wake up some morning back in our campsite?" Dixon's voice had risen to a shout.

"Is everything all right?"

They turned to find a pale and frightened Rachel leaning against the wall for support. Elizabeth jumped up and was at her side before Dixon could respond.

"You should be in bed. You shouldn't be up moving around. You'll cause your wound to open up and start bleeding again," Elizabeth scolded.

"I heard shouting, and I was worried about you."

A look passed between them that rooted Dixon to the floor. "Come on," Elizabeth said to Rachel. "Let me help you back to bed."

Dixon stood transfixed, unwilling to believe what she had just witnessed. When Elizabeth returned Dixon pounced. "You're in love with her," she blurted, her anger quickly replacing reason. "Is she the reason for your newfound *whole*ness? Is that it?"

"Please, stop screaming."

"Jesus Christ! That's it, isn't it!" Dixon's voice had fallen to a raw whisper, but her loss of volume was from shock, not compliance with Elizabeth's request. She slid to the floor and rested her head against her knees. Her jeans quickly absorbed the falling tears.

"Dix." Elizabeth knelt beside her and wrapped her arms around her.

Dixon tried to pull away, but Elizabeth held her as sobs racked Dixon's body. Elizabeth continued holding her until there were no more tears and a sleep born of exhaustion overtook Dixon.

CHAPTER FOUR

Dixon woke before daylight. She had been wrapped in quilts and left on the floor before the fireplace. Elizabeth was nowhere in sight. *Is she with Rachel?* Dixon wondered. She considered checking the bedroom but was afraid of what she might find. Instead she slunk out of the house and walked to the slope where the tunnel had been.

She sat on a boulder and stared at the solid rock wall, not wanting to think about Elizabeth and Rachel but unable to think of anything else.

Elizabeth found her there several hours later. "I

thought I might find you here," Elizabeth said, taking a seat on a rock near Dixon. "I brought you a sandwich and a canteen of water."

"I'm not hungry," Dixon snapped, knowing she sounded like a petulant child.

Elizabeth set the food and water aside. "Dixon, we have to talk."

"Shouldn't you be down there with your new lover? Or has it not reached that stage yet?"

When Elizabeth didn't respond, Dixon ventured a glance in her direction. Elizabeth was looking out over the valley, but the trembling of her shoulders told Dixon she was crying. Dixon wanted to reach for her and make everything better, but she feared her touch wouldn't be welcomed. She was being a total ass, but she couldn't stop how she felt.

"Why can't you just be happy for me?" Elizabeth demanded. Without waiting for an answer, she stood and walked away.

Tears stained Dixon's face as she watched Elizabeth leave. Would this nightmare never end?

A pattern developed over the next two weeks. Dixon would leave the house early each morning. During the first week Elizabeth would get up and insist Dixon have breakfast before she left. Elizabeth continued to treat Dixon as she always had, but Dixon didn't feel comfortable being around them. When Rachel was strong enough to start joining them for breakfast, Dixon made it a point to be out of the house before they got up. She convinced herself that they were confused on where the tunnel had been and wandered the area around the slope searching fruitlessly for it.

After the first week, she gave up searching and sat for hours each day, staring at the spot where the tunnel should have been. Elizabeth came up several times to beg Dixon to return to the house, but Dixon refused. Elizabeth had finally given up and left her alone.

Rachel was much better by the second week and would still be up when Dixon returned for supper. After the second night of having to watch their discreet but meaningful looks, Dixon packed some provisions and left Elizabeth a note stating she would be camping by the tunnel in case it reappeared during the night. Her entire existence now depended on the tunnel reopening. If she could get Elizabeth away from this nightmare, she would forget about Rachel and everything would be fine. Elizabeth would love her as she had before. Dixon neglected to remind herself that she had not been satisfied with the level of Elizabeth's love before entering the tunnel.

Dixon only returned to the stage station to replenish her food and water supply, always fearful that the tunnel would open while she was gone and that she would miss it. When she could no longer stand her own dirt, she bathed and washed her single set of clothes in the stream in the valley below the tunnel. Obsession became a way of life for her. With time away from Rachel and Elizabeth, Dixon rationalized the affair, as she now thought of it. Rachel was a beautiful woman and Elizabeth had saved her life. Elizabeth was simply enchanted by Rachel and was under some type of spell in this time-dimension madness. Dixon just needed to get Elizabeth home, and everything would be fine.

Dixon was surprised to see Rachel coming up the slope late one afternoon.

"Hello," Rachel called in a clear voice as she approached Dixon's makeshift tent.

"What do you want?" Dixon asked, not bothering to hide her hostility.

"I came to talk to you. Elizabeth is very sad, and this sadness isn't good for her or the child."

Dixon had almost forgotten about Elizabeth's pregnancy. "Is she sick?" she asked, suddenly frightened.

"Only her heart," Rachel replied, kneeling beside her. She still wore the same blue dress but had covered the ripped bodice by wearing the man's faded blue shirt that Dixon had seen hanging over the chair.

Dixon looked away, biting back an angry retort about hearts being broken.

"Dixon, I don't understand what is happening here nor do I understand your world. It's more than I can even imagine, but Liz has told me so many things that I can no longer doubt it exists."

Dixon cringed at the use of the shortened version of Elizabeth's name. She was the only person who had ever been allowed that honor. That was one more thing Rachel had changed.

When Dixon made no response, she continued. "I have always known I was" she faltered — "different from other women. I married Benjamin because his father owned land next to my father's. Our union was beneficial to both of us. I was an only child. My mother died when I was quite young. When my father died after Benjamin and I were married, everything that would have been mine, had I been a man, went

56

under Benjamin's control. He was very strict, but not a cruel husband. I was" — she hesitated — "content with Benjamin. But I was never as happy and starry-eyed as my girlfriends were with their new husbands. I thought something was wrong with me. That there was some flaw in my character that prevented me from loving."

She wrapped a tendril of hair that had escaped from the ivory clip back behind her ear. "I now understand. Liz has helped me discover an answer to my difference, and I want to make a new life with her."

Her words tore through Dixon, but she was unable to move or stop listening.

"I feel as though I have been waiting for her my whole life." She extended a hand toward Dixon, who twisted away from her touch. "I know you love her also," she added.

"I guess the two of you have had a pretty good laugh over that," Dixon snapped, knowing she was being childish.

"Liz has never mentioned it. I saw it in your eyes."

Dixon looked away, feeling as if she had just been caught in some terrible shame.

"My father was a widely-read man, and he often told me there are people who, for some reason or other, can never find happiness, no matter what they do. He believed these people had somehow been born in the wrong place or time. I believe Liz was born too late. I know in my heart that Liz and I were meant to be together."

Elizabeth's words burned into Dixon's mind. *"I'm whole,"* she had said.

"Dixon, you and Liz share a bond that can never be broken." Rachel glanced away. "I would never try to compete with or lessen that love." She took a deep breath and turned back to her. "I believe deep in your heart that you know the love you are searching for is not to be found with Liz. Please, come back to the house. Liz needs you."

Dixon remained silent and continued to stare at the solid rock wall until Rachel's footsteps disappeared down the slope. She fluctuated between anger and feeling like a horse's ass. She continued to sit as the sun slid behind the horizon. She didn't notice the sharply dropping temperatures that arrived with the darkness.

Rachel's words continued to race through her thoughts. Elizabeth had said practically the same thing. Was she misreading her own love for Elizabeth? She thought back over the years of their friendship. There had definitely been plenty of times she had been sexually attracted to Elizabeth, but was that love speaking or the thrill of the unattainable? Would Elizabeth have been so desirable if she hadn't pushed Dixon away? Dixon squirmed uncomfortably. Had she used her feelings for Elizabeth to extricate herself from relationships that she shouldn't have become involved in to begin with? The night chill ripped through her. She wrapped herself in a double layer of quilts and sat staring at the stars. She continued to debate her emotions until the pink dawn crept over the mountains.

Exhausted but finally clear in her feelings, she made her way to the stage station to apologize.

Through the window she watched Elizabeth

reflected in the lamplight. She sat at the table watching Rachel, who was standing by the fireplace. Dixon stepped closer and saw Rachel turn and smile at something Elizabeth had said. Elizabeth stood and embraced her. They shared a soft kiss. Dixon waited for the sharp, excruciating pain of betrayal to rip through her. When it didn't, she made her way to the cabin and knocked on the door.

"I've been thinking," Elizabeth said as Dixon brought in the bucket of water from the pump. Elizabeth's shirt was starting to strain over her protruding abdomen.

"What about?" she asked, pouring water into a pitcher that Rachel held.

"According to the stage logs I found under the bar, the stage comes through here once a month." She looked up at Dixon. "I think the stage and the tunnel are connected somehow."

Dixon twisted sharply and poured water down the front of Rachel's dress and onto the floor.

"Are you sure?" she asked, ignoring Elizabeth and Rachel's attempts to clean up her mess.

Elizabeth shrugged as she handed the wet rags to Rachel. "It's no more than a hunch, but I think it's worth checking."

"When will the stage be through again?" Dixon asked, barely breathing.

"Next Wednesday, if it's on time."

"It's always on time," Rachel replied. "The Butterfield Line prides itself on being on time."

* * * * *

For the next six days all Dixon could talk or think about was their crawling back through the tunnel. On the night before the stage was due, Rachel pleaded exhaustion and slipped off to bed early.

"How do you think she will adjust to the twentieth century?" Dixon asked after Rachel left.

Elizabeth laid the shirt she had been mending aside. Dixon still marveled at the skills Elizabeth had picked up after crawling through the tunnel, while all Dixon seemed to be able to do was haul water and split wood — two talents she possessed *before* crawling through.

"She won't have to," Elizabeth answered quietly.

Dixon stared in disbelief. "She's not going back with us?"

Elizabeth shook her head.

Dixon felt her heart go out to her dear friend. Elizabeth would be devastated without Rachel. They had been careful not to deliberately show displays of affection in front of her, but Dixon could see the look of love in Elizabeth's eyes when she looked at Rachel, and the thin walls had not blocked the soft moans and the muffled squeak of the bed coming from their room at night. Dixon had gradually grown fond of Rachel's quiet ways.

"I'm sure we can convince her to change her mind in the morning," Dixon persisted.

"No. It would be too complicated. Besides, Rachel wouldn't be any happier than I was."

"We can find ways to get her . . ." Dixon's words choked off as a thought beyond comprehension came to her. "You don't intend to stay here, do you?"

Elizabeth's look told her that was exactly what she intended.

Dixon jumped up. "No! I won't let you. You don't belong here. Think of the baby," she reasoned. "What if you get sick or there are complications during birth?"

Elizabeth placed her hand on Dixon's arm. "I don't want to go back," she said tenderly. "This is where I belong. Please, try to understand." She smiled and added, "I'll be fine, and I know the baby's all right. I feel great."

"What about me?" Dixon demanded.

"You'll be fine. You're the strongest, bravest person I've ever known, remember?" Her voice broke, and tears crowded the corner of her eyes.

Dixon's throat closed on her own tears. She wanted to argue, but she could see that Elizabeth's mind was made up. If the tunnel reappeared tomorrow, she would be returning alone.

The two friends were still sitting at the table holding hands when Rachel came in the next morning. She quietly made breakfast as they sat watching their time together tick away. None of them was able to eat. After several minutes of pushing their food around on their plates, they made their way up the slope.

Dixon's stomach felt as though she had been eating rocks. Unable to stand still, she finished off the remaining exposures on the roll of film with shots of Elizabeth and Rachel. After removing the roll from the camera, she slid it into her pants pocket along with the one she had taken on the day she and Elizabeth had left camp. She set the camera on a slab of rock and clung to Elizabeth's hand.

The sun had already passed its midpoint range when they saw the first signs of dust.

"It's coming," Rachel said, as they all turned to stare at the solid mountainside.

"Nothing's happening," Dixon said, feeling a strange mixture of apprehension and elation.

"Wait until the stage comes into sight," Elizabeth directed. "It wasn't that far away when we crawled through."

They turned to watch the distant trail of dust until at last the stage began to take shape. They turned as one to find the tunnel before them where a solid limestone wall had been only moments ago. They stared in disbelief.

Elizabeth spoke first. "You'll have to hurry." Rachel gave Dixon a quick, shy hug before breaking away. Elizabeth ran with Dixon to the tunnel, and for a moment they contemplated each other, knowing this parting would be forever. "Look for me in the history books," Elizabeth said through her tears.

"Take care of yourself," Dixon ordered and swallowed her tears. She pressed her hands against Elizabeth's abdomen and said, "Good luck with Elizabeth Junior here."

"Dixon Junior," she replied. She grabbed Dixon's hand. "Listen to me. I've been thinking about this, and I want you to do something for me. Go to the Alamo where we first met, exactly one year from today, May first? Be by the fishpond at precisely 11:00 A.M. Will you do that for me?"

Dixon nodded. She would have promised anything at this point.

"Promise," Elizabeth demanded.

"Pinkie swear," Dixon choked.

No longer able to hold back the tears, they clung to each other. Dixon could hear the faint rattling of the stage. They turned together to look at it.

The stage was drawing near the pass. It would soon be at the stage station. "Go," Elizabeth said, pushing her forward.

Dixon gave Elizabeth's hand one final squeeze, grabbed her camera, and swung it around her neck. Scrambling into the tunnel she began to crawl. She was over halfway through when the back of her jeans caught on something above her. She tried to pull herself free, but whatever she was caught on refused to give.

"What's wrong?" she heard Elizabeth calling to her.

"I'm caught on something." Dixon was beginning to panic. The camera pulled at her neck. She yanked it off and tossed it behind her.

And then Elizabeth was behind her, struggling with the back of her jeans. Dust was beginning to trickle down on them. Dixon felt her panic turn to terror as the dust changed to pebbles.

"It's collapsing," Dixon yelled, "get out!" There was a sharp tug of her waistband. She heard the material of her jeans rip and then Elizabeth pushed her.

"Hurry, Dixon!" she screamed.

Dixon scrambled forward, heedless of the sharp rocks that tore into her hands and knees and of the debris that was rapidly becoming larger and falling down around her. She kept trying to see what happened to Elizabeth, but the tunnel was too small for her to turn around in. She screamed Elizabeth's name and continued to crawl. Dixon thought she heard Elizabeth respond once, but another large rock fell somewhere behind her and sent her racing through the opening. Small rocks pelted down on her as she burst out onto the side of the slope and tumbled down hill. Dust and debris hailed down on her. It sounded as though the entire mountain was collapsing. Dixon's body continued to tumble until it slammed against a slab of rock, knocking her breath from her. She gasped until she could again breathe, but a sharp stabbing pain pierced her side. She struggled to stand up. Had Elizabeth made it out of the tunnel on this side? Or had she crawled back out on the other side? Dixon tried to take a step, but her knees buckled and blackness engulfed her.

CHAPTER FIVE

Dixon opened her eyes to the cold sterility of a hospital room. She sat up, calling for Elizabeth. A sharp pain stabbed her side, and the room spun in a crazy whirl. A nurse appeared and attempted to push her back onto the bed, but Dixon kept fighting to get up. A pair of warm, strong hands pressed her firmly but gently back onto the bed. A heavyset woman with short, gray hair was leaning over her and talking. The soothing tone of her voice calmed Dixon until she gradually relaxed.

"I'm Dr. Gorman. You're in the hospital at Carlsbad," the woman said.

"Did Elizabeth make it out? Did she make it back to Rachel?" She was clinging to the doctor's arm.

"Rachel? Was someone else with you and Ms. Colter?" the doctor asked as she shot a look at the nurse who shook her head. The doctor's frown disappeared. "Ms. Hayes, you've been through quite an ordeal. You and Ms. Colter were missing for a month. There has been a massive search effort. You're going to be all right, but you need to rest." She was studying the monitors that were connected to Dixon. "Your vital signs are good, but you've had a smack on your head, two cracked ribs —"

Dixon interrupted. She didn't care about herself, she needed to know about Elizabeth. "Do you know anything about Elizabeth?"

The doctor gave a weary sigh. "I'm sorry. We don't know anything for certain at this time. All we know for sure is that a small earthquake triggered the landslide you were caught in and that a group of hikers found you at the edge of it. There was no sign of Ms. Colter. Due to the size of the slide and the impossibility of getting heavy equipment into the area, it will be some time before rescue workers can dig through the rubble. They are working as quickly as they can."

"She made it back to the other side," Dixon said. "She had to."

"It's the sedative," she heard the doctor whisper to the nurse as sleep crept back to claim Dixon.

* * * * *

Dixon woke to find her mother and Elizabeth's sister, Jennifer, sitting by her bed. They both looked exhausted.

"Elizabeth?" Dixon asked without thinking.

They both came to stand by her. Mrs. Hayes immediately began to fuss with the sheets, her chin trembling dangerously.

"Mom, I'm okay," Dixon tried to reassure her mother. Mrs. Hayes was overprotective. If Dixon gave her the slightest opportunity, Mrs. Hayes would start insisting that Dixon needed someone to take care of her. Then she would be moving in with Dixon. And although Dixon loved her mother, she could not live with her. Dixon turned to Jennifer. "Elizabeth?" she repeated.

"They're still looking," Jennifer answered, blinking away her own tears.

"She's okay." Dixon squeezed Jennifer's hand. How could she explain to her without sounding like a mental case that Elizabeth was on the other side of the mountain slope, living in another time dimension? Dixon watched as Jennifer's face assumed its professional demeanor. Ten years of emergency medicine had taught her how to turn off her emotions.

Mrs. Hayes leaned closer to stroke Dixon's hair. "We'll have you home in no time. I'll stay with you until you're able to get around. I'll call your Aunt Katie and ask her to mail me some more of my clothes. As soon as you're feeling better, we can go back home and you can stay with me. You'll have to take it easy for a while. No more traipsing around the country taking pictures."

Dixon closed her eyes and groaned.

"Now, now. Don't you worry," Mrs. Hayes said and patted Dixon's hand. "I draw enough from your father's social security and his pension plan for us to live comfortably."

"Mom, please," Dixon pleaded.

Jennifer quickly stepped in. "Rose, you've been sitting here for hours. Why don't you go have something to eat and let me sit with Dixon for a while? You shouldn't wear yourself out."

"I can't leave."

Dixon needed to talk to Jennifer alone. "Mom, I'm fine," Dixon assured her. "Go eat so I won't be worried about you. You know the doctor told you to watch your blood sugar."

At the mention of one of her numerous conditions, Mrs. Hayes tugged at the top of her mulberry-colored jogging suit. She had started wearing jogging suits after Dixon's father had died, and now she rarely wore anything else. "I wouldn't be much good to you ill, now would I?" she agreed, reaching beneath the bed and retrieving a purse that was larger than Dixon's camera equipment bag. "I'll have to force myself to eat, but for you honey, anything." She gave Dixon's face a gentle pat before she scurried off.

Dixon smiled as she watched the plump figure of her mother disappear out the door.

"We almost had to twist her arm," Jennifer said smiling.

They stared at each other for a moment before Jennifer took Dixon's hand. "I know this is hard," she began, "but if you're up to it, I need to know what happened."

Now that they were alone, Dixon wasn't sure what to say. She turned away as her own list of questions began to assault her. How could she tell Jennifer the truth? What would Elizabeth want Jennifer to know? How long would the rescue teams continue to look for Elizabeth's body? What would happen when it wasn't found? She wished desperately that she and Elizabeth had talked about what would happen when Dixon returned alone.

Jennifer squeezed her hand. Dixon turned to look into brown eyes that were shadowed with exhaustion. "All I can tell you is that Elizabeth has found happiness."

A frown creased Jennifer's forehead. "What do you mean?" Her eyes suddenly sparked with anger. "Are you trying to tell me Elizabeth preferred death to living?"

"No!" Dixon shot up to protest, and the searing pain caused her to cry out. The room spun, and Dixon fought to catch her breath.

"Lie back." Jennifer's face hovered over her.

"She's okay," Dixon managed to whisper, ignoring the look of concern on Jennifer's face.

"I'm sorry I brought it up. You need to rest," Jennifer said crisply. Silence fell between them, and despite her turmoil, Dixon soon drifted off to sleep.

Dixon was released the next day after making her statement to a police officer. Dixon rambled off what she hoped was a believable lie about how they had left the trail and got lost. She swore she could remember nothing about the landslide. She bit her tongue and before he finally left endured a two-minute lecture on the poor judgment they had used in leaving the trail.

After leaving the hospital, she spent two drawn-out, emotionally-exhausting days in a hotel room with her mother. Mrs. Hayes had insisted that Dixon spend most of the time in bed, even though the doctor had told Dixon to move around as much as possible. Mrs. Hayes had practically spoon-fed Dixon her meals.

Dixon knew her mother meant well, but there was no way Dixon could tolerate her constant hovering. Mrs. Hayes had a large circle of friends back in Ohio and was active in several charities. Her mother had always been overly protective, but had got worse after Dixon's father died. It was as though she had taken all of the attention she had once bestowed upon him and transferred it to Dixon. He had never seemed to mind her mother's constant hovering and fussing.

It had taken Dixon most of the two days to convince her mother to return to Ohio alone. Mrs. Hayes sniffed all the way to the airport, fiercely protesting that she should accompany Dixon back to San Antonio. Dixon remained adamant, knowing that once her mother was entrenched in Dixon's apartment, it would take a battalion of Marines to remove her.

Dixon held her breath as her mother's plane left the ground. She watched the silver speck until it was completely out of sight, somehow fearing that at any moment her mother would make them turn the plane around and let her off. When it didn't reappear, she breathed a sigh of relief and made her way toward the coffee shop to await her own plane. Jennifer had decided to stay until the search team either found Elizabeth's body or gave up the attempt. Dixon felt guilty leaving her, but she was sure Elizabeth had made it back. When Dr. Gorman had expressed some concerns about Dixon driving back to San Antonio alone, Mrs. Hayes had quickly assured her she was available to help drive back. Dixon had pled fatigue and said she wanted to fly home. She could always come back for the car later. Jennifer had saved the day by offering to drive Dixon's car back to San Antonio when she left.

It was after midnight when Dixon arrived at her apartment. Her mail was in a neat stack on the coffee table, and a pile of handwritten messages was beside the answering machine. Mrs. Jenkins, her neighbor and sometimes unofficial personal assistant, had been watching the place and feeding her tropical fish. A quick glance at the aquarium verified that her small family had all survived her absence. Careful of her ribs, she slipped into her favorite chair and ignored the mail and messages. There was no one she wanted to see or talk to.

She listened to the slow gurgling of the aquarium's pump and thought about the last time that she had sat there. She had been planning the great weekend she and Elizabeth would have. Realization struck. She would never again be able to see or talk to her dear friend. She cried herself to sleep.

Dixon woke to darkness, stiff from sleeping in the chair. She stumbled to her bed. The red glare of the digital clock told her it was after 3:00. It was almost eighteen hours later when the phone woke her again.

Dixon felt hungover from the long sleep. She fumbled for the phone in the dark, knowing it was her mother checking on her.

"Hello," she rasped, trying to keep her eyes open.

"Dixon," a strangled voice said, "this is Jennifer."

Dixon sat up sharply and winced at the pain in her side.

"I just got into San Antonio and wanted to be the one to let you know. They found Elizabeth's body right after you left. I didn't call sooner, because . . . it took a while to identify the body."

The words slammed into Dixon, but she couldn't understand them. How could they find Elizabeth's body? She was with Rachel. Comprehension hit her. Elizabeth hadn't made it out of the tunnel after helping her escape. A primal scream tore from her throat as she jumped from bed, ripped the phone from the wall, and flung it across the floor. "It's not fair," she screamed over and over. She had been the one who had insisted on crawling into the tunnel originally. Elizabeth had been afraid. "Why didn't I listen," she shouted. She pounded her fist against her forehead. "It's all my fault."

Jennifer and Mrs. Jenkins found her half an hour later, a sobbing mass huddled in the corner by the aquarium.

"Dixon." Jennifer's voice sliced through her pain.

"Let us help you up, dear," Mrs. Jenkins said, taking her by the arm. Together they managed to get her onto the sofa.

"I'll get her a glass of water," Mrs. Jenkins said and scurried off.

Dixon kept visualizing how terrified Elizabeth must have been as the tunnel walls collapsed around her. Over and over again, Dixon heard her own voice scoffing at Elizabeth's fear of the tunnel collapsing on the day they had found it.

"Dixon." Jennifer's tear-stained face loomed in

front of her. Like Elizabeth, Jennifer Stewart was a short, thin-framed woman. She was married, had four boys, and was an emergency medicine doctor at a downtown hospital. Jennifer stroked Dixon's hair back from her face. "Elizabeth wouldn't have wanted you to grieve like this. You've got to get control of yourself. Have you taken any kind of medication?"

"It was my fault." Dixon hiccuped. "She didn't even like to camp. She didn't want me to crawl through. She kept telling me we should stay on the path. Everybody knows you don't leave the trails."

"Dixon, listen to me." Jennifer wiped at Dixon's face with a tissue. "I'm going to give you a sedative, but I need to know if you've taken any other medication. Did they give you anything when you left the hospital?"

Dixon managed to shake her head no before she was seized by chills. "She was safe. My jeans got caught on something. She came in to help me and then pushed me out of the way." She grabbed Jennifer's thin shoulders. "I thought she got out the other side." Dixon barely felt the sting of the needle. Jennifer squeezed her hand.

"No one's blaming you."

"You should. It's my fault!" What had happened to Rachel? Dixon couldn't fathom the pain Rachel must have felt when Elizabeth hadn't come back. And it was all Dixon's fault. If she had just been more careful. If she hadn't dragged Elizabeth on that damn camping trip.

Mrs. Jenkins's hefty form returned with the water and a wet cloth. "Drink this and let me wipe your face, child."

Dixon tried to drink the water, but it wouldn't go

past the massive lump in her throat. She began to choke. She was aware of Mrs. Jenkins rubbing her back as Jennifer sat her up. Then the warm cloth was running over her face, and Jennifer was again holding her hand as the sedative took effect.

Dixon woke to a stream of sunshine across her face. Jennifer was sleeping soundly in the chair next to the sofa with an afghan thrown over her. The clock on the wall said it was 7:30. Dixon felt as though she had been sleeping for days. As Dixon eased her feet off the sofa, Jennifer's eyes shot open.

"I'm sorry I woke you," Dixon rasped, her voice heavy.

"Four kids give you a built-in motion detector," Jennifer said lightly as she moved next to her and checked her pulse. "How are you feeling?"

"Like someone packed my head with cotton. I need a shower." With Jennifer's help, Dixon made it into the bathroom.

"I'll be fine," Dixon said, gripping the door frame.

"Are you sure?"

"Yeah."

"I'll fix us something to eat."

As Dixon stripped off her jeans, a canister of film fell out of her pocket. She bent carefully, picked it up and tossed it into the trash can. The scenery of the Guadalupe Mountains National Park no longer appealed to her.

She stepped into the shower, and let the water pound down on her head until the cobwebs began to clear. When memories crowded in and threatened to overwhelm her, she recited the multiplication tables through sixteen and then started saying her ABC's backward. Anything to keep from thinking about Elizabeth and Rachel. What had happened to Rachel? Dixon began on the multiplication tables again as she stepped out of the shower.

A bowl of soup and a tuna sandwich were waiting for her when Dixon returned. Dixon felt her stomach churn at the sight of food. She sat down and pushed the food away.

"You need to eat something," Jennifer stated.

"Just coffee," Dixon insisted.

"You can have coffee after you eat."

Too tired to argue, Dixon pulled the soup to her and sipped a spoonful of the broth. When it stayed down she tried another sip, while Jennifer ate the sandwich. They ate in silence until Dixon pushed the half-empty bowl of soup away. For the first time she noticed the dark shadows beneath Jennifer's eyes.

"How are you doing?" Dixon asked.

Jennifer shrugged and poured each of them a cup of coffee. "I can't believe I'll never see her again." Tears slid down her face. "I see death every day, but I never think about it happening to someone I love." She took a deep breath and wiped away the tears. "I need to ask you a couple of questions, if you feel up to it." Jennifer was slowly turning her cup in circles.

"I'll tell you anything I can," Dixon promised, still not knowing how she would be able to tell Jennifer the truth.

Jennifer ran her hands over her face. "I called home while you were in the shower. John told me they had called with the results of the autopsy last night. It revealed that Elizabeth was four months pregnant. Did you know?"

Dixon traced the swirl pattern on the tablecloth. "She told me the first night we camped. She said she was afraid to say anything sooner. She knew I'd try to talk her out of it."

An awkward silence fell between them. "What happened out there? How did you two get lost? How did she —" Jennifer's voice broke.

Dixon's heart fought her better judgment. Her heart won. "Let's go back into the living room." She needed time to think. After they were settled side by side on the sofa, Dixon took a long, ragged breath.

"Jennifer, something happened out there, and if I tell you, you'll think I'm crazy. There were times when I doubted my own sanity." She ventured a quick glance at Jennifer before continuing. "I'm sorry, but you have to promise that you'll listen to everything I have to say before you make any type of judgment."

Jennifer gave a somewhat reluctant nod, and Dixon gradually revealed what had happened. When she reached the part about the tunnel caving in she had to stop several times, but at last Jennifer knew the entire story, except for Dixon's promise to be at the fishpond at the Alamo in a year.

Jennifer didn't speak. Dixon remained still, giving her time to process the information.

When Jennifer spoke she was hesitant. "I want to believe you, but it seems so . . ." She let the sentence die.

Dixon turned to face her. "Think about this," she

began. "We left camp with three gallons of water and enough food for lunch. You know they found our backpacks with most of the water and all the food still in them. How do you think we survived out there for a month? Look at me. Do I look like I've been wandering around eating roots and berries for a month?" Seeing a flicker of doubt in Jennifer's eyes, she rushed on. "When they found me I was less than two hundred yards from where they found our backpacks. They said we had been wandering in circles." She scooted closer to Jennifer and grabbed her hands. "I could walk that trail with my eyes closed. Do you honestly believe I could have got so lost that I walked in circles for thirty days without seeing some landmark I recognized? Why didn't we run into other hikers? The park is isolated but not deserted. Why couldn't the rescue teams find us if we were walking in circles?" When Jennifer didn't respond, Dixon pushed on. "It was because we weren't there for them to find until we crawled back through the tunnel."

Jennifer clamped her hands over her ears. "Stop!"

Dixon waited.

"This is too much for me to sort through right now. I have to think about it." She jumped up. "I have to go home. Will you be all right? Mrs. Jenkins would be more than happy to stay with you."

"I'm fine," Dixon said and leaned back on the sofa. She could tell Jennifer didn't believe her. *Can I really blame her?* she asked herself.

Jennifer gathered up her bag and stopped at the door. "Dixon, I want to believe you, and I know in my heart that whatever you tell me you truly believe. Are you sure, absolutely sure, you weren't hallucinating or dreaming or something?"

Dixon didn't answer. Maybe she was crazy.

Jennifer called the next day to check on her and to give her the funeral arrangements. Dixon wrote the information down, crawled back into bed, and cried herself to sleep.

The next two days were a blur of pain for her. Somehow she managed to get herself up and dressed each morning. Mrs. Jenkins came in and cooked breakfast for her and made sure she ate. She saw Jennifer daily, but they never discussed what had happened.

After the funeral and the crowd of mourners had left John and Jennifer's home, Dixon found Jennifer sitting alone in the garden. They had hardly spoken during the past two days, and now there was an uneasy silence between them. "I just came to say good-bye," Dixon said, unsure of how Jennifer felt about her. Did she blame her for Elizabeth's death? *It's only fair if she does*, Dixon told herself. When Jennifer didn't respond, Dixon turned to leave.

"Dixon."

Dixon stopped to look back.

"Elizabeth was truly happy for those last few days?"

"Yes. She was happier than she had ever been. She and Rachel were very happy."

Jennifer stood and walked toward her. "Don't just

disappear. Keep in touch." Jennifer gave her a quick hug.

Dixon nodded, knowing she probably wouldn't.

Dixon went into hibernation in her apartment. She turned the phones off and ignored the doorbell on the two occasions it rang. She slept and mourned for Elizabeth. She blamed herself for her death. If she hadn't insisted on exploring the tunnel. If she had been more careful when she crawled back through. If they had gone somewhere else for their vacation. *If, if, if!* She continued to alternate between tears and self-condemnation. In her dreams and during unguarded moments, she relived the tunnel's collapse a dozen times and carefully replayed those last few minutes with Elizabeth.

After almost two weeks, she woke one morning ready to face the world again. She plugged the phones back in and thoroughly cleaned her apartment.

After a long, hot shower, she stood in front of the mirror, blow drying her black, curly mop of hair, and realized how long it had grown. By late afternoon, she had got it cut, bought groceries, and treated herself to a nice dinner at Lucia's, her favorite Italian restaurant.

Mrs. Jenkins caught her as Dixon was opening the door to her apartment when she returned home.

"There you are, dear," she called as Dixon swung her door open.

She smiled, knowing Mrs. Jenkins had timed her

appearance to the nanosecond. Dixon really did like her, even if she did have a slightly nosy streak.

"I came by a couple of times, and when you didn't answer I knew you weren't ready for company. When my Herb died, all I wanted to do was be alone. So I knew how you felt."

Mrs. Jenkins's husband had died four years before Dixon had moved into this apartment, and she rarely spoke of him. When she did, Dixon could see the love and loneliness in her pale, watery eyes.

"Thank you for allowing me time," Dixon replied, realizing that Mrs. Jenkins had assumed she and Elizabeth were lovers. Dixon had never kept her lifestyle a secret, and Mrs. Jenkins had apparently drawn her own conclusions. "Would you like to come in? I'll put on a pot of coffee."

"No, dear. I'm on my way to the senior's hall. It's Thursday you know."

"Bingo night." Dixon nodded.

"Would you like to join us?"

Dixon almost laughed. She wasn't quite ready for bingo yet. "Not tonight, but thanks anyway."

"All right, but you let me know if you change your mind." She patted her arm. "Oh, I almost forgot why I came over." She held out a small bag of photographs. "I was tidying up for you during the funeral, and I found a couple of rolls of film. One had fallen into the trash, and the other was in your trousers pockets."

Dixon smiled at the word *trouser*. Mrs. Jenkins must have thought she was happy to have had the film processed, because she gave a brief sigh and her smile brightened.

"I know you normally do your own processing, but since these were just vacation pictures, I thought I'd save you some time and drop them off at the drugstore for you."

"Thank you, Mrs. Jenkins. I appreciate your doing that. Come in and let me pay you." Dixon insisted, knowing Mrs. Jenkins's finances were usually tight.

"No, dear, I really have to hurry now. You take care and start getting out more."

"I will," Dixon promised, not sure she meant it.

Mrs. Jenkins tucked the bag of photos in with Dixon's groceries and hurried back to her apartment.

Dixon threw the photos on the table, trying to ignore the bag. She had not wanted to see them. She put away the groceries and made a pot of coffee. When it was ready she sat at the table with a cup and drew the offending bag to her. There would be photos of Elizabeth, the last photos of Elizabeth. She carefully removed the packets from the bag, telling herself she was looking for a receipt so she could reimburse Mrs. Jenkins.

The photos in the first packet contained the spectacular shots of the sunrise she had taken. Dixon flipped through them. Suddenly there was Elizabeth, holding up a hand as she scolded Dixon for taking her picture. There was a series of photos where Elizabeth had given up and started clowning for the camera.

The pain of loss was softer, deeper now, and Dixon sat staring at the photos of her friend for several minutes before reaching for the second pack. There was the magnificent valley they had found after crawling through the tunnel. She flipped rapidly through the shots of the stage station until she found the ones of Elizabeth and Rachel. It was real. Dixon held the photos and stared at them until the phone jarred her back.

It was Alice Mabrey calling. Alice was a photographer Dixon had worked with two years before on a shoot in Africa. Alice worked for a firm that specialized in shooting archaeological digs. She quickly got to the point.

"We're unexpectedly short a photographer for an enormous dig in Missouri. It's in a rather isolated area, and we'll be spending all of our time on location, which means we'll be living in tents, so I knew you'd love it. The job is scheduled for nine to ten months. The financing is coming from a private enterprise that wants the dig cleared so they can get on with whatever it was they were doing, and the pay is sinfully high." She rushed on. "The only catch is the plane leaves in about seven hours. Is your tetanus shot up to date?"

Dixon smiled. This was perfect. A lot of work that was away from everything familiar. She always worked with two cameras and was now short having lost one in the tunnel, but she could make do until she could replace it.

"My shots are current and my bags are packed. Give me the details," she said and grabbed a pencil.

Six hours later as she left her apartment, she slipped an envelope under Mrs. Jenkins's door with a note about where she was going, money to cover the film processing, and a check that covered her household expenses for three months. She would send more later, when needed. She dropped a second envelope into the mailbox for Jennifer. In it was a photo of the stage station and one of Elizabeth and Rachel. An hour and a half later, Dixon was on a plane headed for a new job.

CHAPTER SIX

The plane landed in Saint Louis after midnight. Alice had met Dixon at the airport in San Antonio and had promptly fallen asleep after takeoff. Dixon knew she should try to sleep, but she kept wondering what Jennifer's reaction would be to the photos. Would she believe her now? *Maybe I should call her in a few days,* she thought. *No,* she decided quickly, *I will let Jennifer contact me.*

At this late hour, the Saint Louis airport was lacking its usual daytime hustle, and they were able to claim their luggage quickly.

They had no problems getting a cab and were soon headed for the hotel where reservations had been arranged for the dig team members.

Alice shifted nervously in her seat. "I wanted to let you know, I'm glad you're okay, and I'm real sorry about your friend."

Dixon stared at her. She hadn't thought about other people knowing about the accident. Her loss felt too personal to share. "How did you hear?" she asked, surprised at how normal her voice sounded.

"Damn, woman. It was on the news practically every day. One of the local television stations did a series of interviews with some of the kids from the school where your friend taught. Those kids sure did like her."

Dixon stared out the window. She hadn't thought about how other people would be affected by Elizabeth's death. People Dixon didn't know. It felt strange to realize that Elizabeth had a life that Dixon knew nothing about. Could anyone ever really know someone else?

Alice moved sideways in the seat, and Dixon knew she was staring at her.

"Listen, I understand. And if there's anything I can do," Alice said and then hesitated. Dixon continued to stare out the window. Alice struggled to continue. "What I mean is, while we were working together in Africa, I kind of got the impression you played on the other side of the fence."

"What?" Confused, Dixon turned her gaze back to Alice.

Alice fumbled with a cigarette and glared at the NO SMOKING sign on the dash. "Your lifestyle. It's okay with me," she rushed on. "Hell, the less competition the better, I say." She tapped the cigarette back into the pack. "I just wanted you to know I'm sorry about your friend."

"We weren't lovers," Dixon said, rubbing her hand across her face. Why did everyone think they were lovers? Had Jennifer thought they were? Could she be angry about that? Dixon shook her head to clear away the thought. Jennifer had known about Elizabeth's lifestyle for years, and it had never been an issue. Dixon had been included in dozens of their family gatherings.

Alice cut into her musing. "Oh. I thought . . ."

Dixon sighed. She didn't want to talk about this. "Alice, I'm a lesbian, but Elizabeth and I were only friends." The cab driver was gawking at her in the rearview mirror, and Dixon had a childish urge to stick her tongue out at him.

"Oh," Alice said again.

"This is your hotel," the driver announced a moment later, saving them from further discussion.

Dixon left the briefing disgusted. The private enterprise had turned out to be not so private. It was the Army Corps of Engineers. They had discovered a large Indian burial mound while repairing a levee in a remote area on the Mississippi River. The burial mound had been badly damaged during the recent flooding. The repair crew had immediately stopped working, and an independent team of archaeologists had been contracted by the state to excavate the site, much to the disgust of the commander-in-charge of the levee repair, Colonel Thomas C. Oliver. He had argued persuasively that the damaged levee posed a life-threatening condition if the river flooded, and he had managed to get himself placed in charge of the overall task of ensuring that the team did nothing to drastically increase the damage to the levee.

The morning after Dixon and Alice arrived, he called everyone into a meeting at 9:00 and informed them that he would be supervising the dig. The archaeologists immediately began to protest. He had ignored them and had begun ticking off a list of rules and regulations that sent the entire room into an uproar.

"The arrogant old bastard," Alice seethed next to her. "Who the hell does he think he is anyway?"

Dixon smiled slightly, wondering if Alice was more angry with the colonel's decree that strict house-keeping would be maintained at the site at all times, or that there would be no hanky-panky.

"Tents designated for men only means exactly that," he had warned as he glared at the four women members of the twelve-person team.

Dixon had not protested anything until she heard that she and the other three women would be sharing a tent. She had assumed they would have separate quarters, even if they were tents. She had waited until after the briefing and approached Colonel Oliver. He was meticulously arranging his notes and the stack of contracts they had all signed earlier. He never looked up. "Speak?"

After curbing the urge to bark at him, Dixon said, "My name's Dixon Hayes. I'm one of the photographers, and I'll be taking my own tent along rather than sharing." Dixon had already decided it would be better to buy a tent than have to live with three other people for nine months.

"No, you will not," he declared without looking at her. "You will sleep where you have been assigned."

Dixon's temper flared. "Look, in case you haven't noticed, I don't belong to your little kingdom of soldiers."

He stopped and pierced her with hard, dark eyes. "Miss Hayes, you have signed a contract that was very clear in what you are entitled to, right down to housing." He waved the stack of papers at her. "You have flown here at the government's expense, and you have received a night's lodging courtesy of the same." He gave a thin, humorless smile. "So, yes, you do belong to my 'little kingdom of soldiers' until you have completed your commitment." He turned back to his papers.

Dixon felt her face burn. She hadn't read the entire contract. She had simply verified the length of the contracted time and her salary. "I'm not asking you to pay for my request," she said tightly. "I'll buy everything myself."

He stopped again and turned to her, addressing her as though she were a willful child. "Miss Hayes, if I allow you to do as you please, then eleven other people will feel they are entitled to do so. Within a week there would be complete chaos, and that I will not tolerate. Good night." He strode away, leaving Dixon staring after him.

In less than an hour, they were herded on to a military bus. Dixon chose a spot well away from the six or so men already on the bus. She wanted to be alone with her thoughts. It would take her a while to adjust to being with people constantly. Her solitude was short-lived when Alice and the other two women came back to join her.

"Dixon," Alice called, sliding into the seat in front of her, "meet Doctors Susan Brown and Leanne McQuinness."

"Sue," said the older woman, extending her hand. Dixon quickly took in the short, rounded features of the woman. She was known to be one of the country's leading authorities on Mississippian Indian culture. Alice had told Dixon earlier that Susan and her husband, Darrell, would be members of the dig. Alice had worked with them both on previous digs. In fact, it seemed to Dixon that Alice had worked with everyone on one site or another. Dixon shook Sue's hand. As her hand was pulled away from Sue, it was quickly recaptured.

"Nice to meet you," Leanne McQuinness said as she caught Dixon's retreating hand.

Dixon was drawn into a pair of warm, brown eyes. Leanne smiled, revealing a set of dimples that Dixon had a wild urge to trace with her tongue. Her heart gave a series of erratic flutters as Leanne's warm, soft hand closed around her own and gently squeezed. Dixon's imagination ran rampant through Leanne's long hair, which was now securely fastened in a tight braid. How would it look down, or spread across a pillow, or over thighs that . . . ? She shook off the image and realized with a start that she was still clinging to Leanne's hand. She quickly released it and turned to find Alice watching her, a crooked smile playing across her lips.

"What did you all think of our little Napoleon?" Sue asked, taking the seat across the aisle from Alice. Dixon detected a slight Southern twang in her speech.

"I think he's in a for a long, disappointing haul," Leanne answered in a smooth, quiet voice.

"Do you know he told Ralph no alcohol would be allowed on site?" Alice said, inhaling deeply on her cigarette.

Dixon thought it best not to point out the no smoking sign posted at the front of the bus. She scanned the men sitting up front and chatting quietly among themselves. She tried to recall which of them was Ralph Anderson, the head archaeologist. Her gaze settled on a tall guy with long, gray sideburns and an incredible, bushy mass of hair and remembered Alice introducing her to him. He and Alice had worked together somewhere else.

Sue snorted and brought Dixon's attention back to the conversation. "Ralph's been on more sites than the colonel has rules. What did he say?"

Alice grinned through her cigarette smoke. "He smiled real big and said yes, sir."

"Ralph did?" Leanne asked, surprised. She had stretched out on the seat across from Dixon, who couldn't help but notice her long, tanned, well-muscled body.

Alice's voice stopped the fantasy that Dixon's imagination was about to embark on.

"Yeah, then he and some of the guys went out and bought two extra field trunks and stocked them with prime liquor." Alice laughed a sharp crackling sound common to smokers and nodded at a large stack of trunks and equipment that was being loaded into trucks.

"Well, I'm sure Colonel Oliver will tire of field life much sooner than we will," Leanne said, her eyes slowly raking over Dixon.

Dixon's face began to burn, and she forced herself to open a book she had bought at the San Antonio airport.

Leanne's prediction proved accurate. Colonel Oliver lasted three days, long enough to ensure that the temporary repairs to the levee could handle anything short of a flood. Before departing, he issued a list of strict instructions that Ralph was to enforce. Ralph had walked him to his car and assured him his orders would be followed to the letter. As soon as the colonel's car disappeared, Ralph tossed the list into a trash can, and the team assembled to discuss how the dig would progress.

It was decided they would split into two teams. One team, with Ralph in charge, would start on the north side of the mound, and the other half, headed by Sue, would start on the south side. Alice would act as photographer for Ralph's group and Dixon for Sue's.

Dixon breathed a sigh of relief that Leanne would be working with Ralph. Her long legs and maybe-I-will-maybe-I-won't eyes were too much of a distraction. After a few times of returning to the tent after dinner and finding herself alone with Leanne, Dixon made it a point to hang around the mess tent and play cards with the guys or listen to them recount stories of previous digs, because Leanne always went directly back to the tent to work on her notes.

Dixon tried to analyze why she avoided Leanne. It wasn't as if Leanne had actually said or done anything to suggest she was interested in her. It was something unspoken. Something bubbling just below the surface that Dixon felt each time she looked at or thought about Leanne.

Dixon grabbed her camera and went back to work. She had taken this job to give herself time to get over Elizabeth, not to start a new relationship.

The days melted into weeks. Dixon's team kept her so busy during the day that she barely had time to think as she snapped dozens of shots of recovered artifacts, location sites, and recovery methods. Each roll of film had to be developed on-site in the makeshift darkroom, and meticulous notes had to be kept on each shot. With her demanding workload, it was fairly simple to avoid spending time around Leanne during the day, but the nights were more difficult. There were too many nights when she tossed restlessly on her cot, fully aware that Leanne was only a few feet away from her.

The team had been working for almost three months when the rain started. Not a downpour that would send the colonel scurrying out to check the safety of the levee, but the harmless, slow, steady rain that turned the dig site into an oozing mud pit. And just when Dixon had decided it couldn't get any worse, the sultry heat arrived, followed by swarms of bloodthirsty mosquitoes.

Between the heat, the mud, and the maddening insects, tempers soon flared. No one could get a decent night's sleep, and things had reached a boiling point when Ralph loaded them all on the bus and headed for the nearest motel for five days of rest. Dixon was so ecstatic at the thought of a few days of privacy that she forgot she was avoiding Leanne. Once again the four women sat together and babbled like teenagers. They were headed toward air-conditioning, hot showers with an endless supply of water, real beds, and food that hopefully contained both taste and texture, unlike the strange concoctions the field mess offered.

Ralph went into the Bootheel Motel, the only motel for miles, to arrange for the rooms. He came back with a handful of keys. "Okay, boys and girls," he called as he stepped onto the bus, "listen up. They're in the middle of remodeling and are short on rooms, so we'll have to double up. Grab yourself a roommate and a key."

Dixon groaned. She wouldn't be getting the privacy she had hoped for. She looked up to find Leanne watching her with that strange little smile. Frantic, she turned to Alice to demand they room together, but Alice was busy eyeing Ralph, who was dangling a key at her suggestively. Dixon turned to find Sue, but she was already leaving with her husband, Darrell. Dixon turned back to Leanne.

"Looks like you're stuck with me," Leanne smirked. "Unless, of course, you'd prefer . . ." She nodded toward the milling group of men, one or two of whom were looking toward Dixon and Leanne with a gleam of hope in their eyes.

Dixon mentally reprimanded herself. She was letting her hormones get out of hand. Leanne had done nothing to indicate she was sexually attracted to her. She didn't even know for sure that Leanne was a lesbian. She gave an awkward shrug and followed Leanne to retrieve a key from Ralph. Dixon almost growled at Alice's suggestive wink when she and Leanne stepped off the bus. But her irritation at Alice was soon forgotten as the subtle ripple of muscles beneath Leanne's tight jeans mesmerized Dixon.

The room contained two double beds and a battle-scarred dresser. Everything except the faded blue walls was brown. The room was clean, but beyond that there wasn't much to praise.

"You want to flip for who gets the shower first?" Leanne asked, tossing her bag on the bed near the door. "Unless you'd like to do your part in water conservation and join me."

Dixon's mouth went dry. That definitely sounded like an invitation. She stared at the worn brown carpet, unable to look up. Why did she feel like such a bumbling fool? It wasn't as if she'd never slept with a woman. And Leanne was certainly desirable . . .

"Well?"

"No," Dixon stuttered, "that's fine."

"No what? The toss or water conservation?" Leanne's voice had slipped into a low and seductive drawl. She was moving toward Dixon, who kept backing up until she bumped into the dresser. "Why do you keep avoiding me?" Leanne purred, as she brushed her hand lightly over Dixon's dark tangle of curls. "Have I misjudged your . . . ah . . . preference?"

Dixon's breath was coming in shallow gulps. "No. I just don't . . ."

"Is there someone else?" Leanne's fingers moved sensuously up and down Dixon's neck.

"No." Dixon closed her eyes as Leanne's knee

gently but insistently pushed between her legs. Dixon tried to recall the last time she had made love. *Too long*, her throbbing body yelled back.

"I'm not looking for a lifetime commitment. Let's enjoy what the moment has to offer," Leanne said, unbuttoning Dixon's shirt.

In one deft movement Dixon's bra was loose and on the floor beside her shirt. The breeze from the air conditioner caused her already taut nipples to tighten more. Dixon opened her eyes to find Leanne staring at her hungrily.

"If you don't want this, all you have to do is say stop," Leanne said.

While her brain was screaming, *Stop! I don't even know you*, her body was beyond stopping. Dixon's hand slid behind Leanne's neck and pulled her into a deep, lingering kiss. Dixon's hand moved slowly to allow the wonderful sensations of those first few touches to linger and permeate her.

Leanne's hands tightened around Dixon's hips and pulled her tighter as their jeans-clad bodies struggled to get closer. Their kiss deepened, and their movements became more frantic. Leanne's hands closed around Dixon's breasts and began to massage the swollen nipples. Dixon dug at Leanne's shirt until it was free of her jeans. Their tongues continued their intricate dance. Dixon, clumsy with want, struggled with Leanne's bra clasp until at last it came loose and freed its pendulous captives. Dixon filled her hands with the warm softness and felt her passion mounting.

Leanne's mouth broke away and claimed one of Dixon's aching nipples. Dixon cried out and pushed frantically against Leanne. In one swift move, Leanne unfastened Dixon's jeans and jerked them down her legs. Dixon felt herself being lifted onto the dresser. Leanne's head pushed between Dixon's legs, devouring her.

The waves of sensations started deep in Dixon's center and washed upward until Dixon cried out. The scarred dresser rocked wildly beneath her as her hands locked around Leanne's head and rode the crashing waves of pleasure.

They spent most of the next three days in bed, only leaving when they went to eat and then only to venture no farther than the motel diner.

They were finally forced to leave the motel when Alice called and invited them to meet Ralph and her for dinner at a local restaurant. "You can't miss it," Alice had assured them. "Other than the motel diner, it's the only restaurant in town."

Dixon and Leanne stepped from the cool of the motel room into the heavy humidity, which instantly left them feeling drenched.

"How can anyone stand to live in this humidity?" Leanne moaned. She pulled her braided hair away from her neck.

Dixon smiled to herself. The dig team was made up of individuals from all over the United States. It seemed as though weather was always a major topic for them.

"Some people would ask how anyone could get used to living in those temperatures you get in Arizona," Dixon reminded her.

"But it's not this bad," Leanne assured her and pulled Dixon's shirt away from her back. "Look at your shirt. It's already soaked, and we've just stepped out."

"You didn't mind sweating earlier," Dixon reminded her.

Leanne's eyes sparkled. "I wouldn't mind sweating now, if I had a good reason."

Dixon felt the slow burn begin and shook her head. No one had ever affected her the way Leanne did with that unquenchable sense of raw sexuality. "How do you do that?" Dixon asked.

"I'm not doing anything," Leanne assured her in a voice that was definitely doing something.

"Let's call Alice and plead heat exhaustion," Dixon said, twisting her fingers into the belt loops on Leanne's shorts.

Leanne laughed. "Forget it. I'm starved."

They strolled through the small town that consisted of a hardware store, a small grocery store, two gas stations, the restaurant, the motel, and a junk/secondhand store. Dixon felt a certain amount of envy for the people who lived here. They probably knew everyone in town, and their families had probably known one another for years. *They also know everybody's business*, she reminded herself and again appreciated the anonymity of a big city.

Alice and Ralph were waiting for them inside the small restaurant. If it favored a particular decor, Dixon was unable to spot it. What it did emit was the wonderful smell of fresh bread. Dixon breathed in deeply. Fresh bread was a weakness of hers. She already knew she would be stuffed by the time she left.

At Alice's insistence, they were led to the smoking section near the back. The hostess seated them, passed out plastic menus, and hurried away. A large vinyl rubber tree plant hid them from most of the room.

"Maybe I should have taken time to shave," Ralph joked as they settled around the worst table in the restaurant. Leanne was seated across from Dixon.

"I think it was Alice's cigarettes." Dixon wrinkled her nose. "Don't you know those things will kill you and everyone around you?"

"Well, we're all going to die anyway," Alice growled and lit a long, brown cigarette.

The waitress appeared to take their orders, and the conversation turned to the site. Dixon was enjoying her salad and the fresh garlic bread that accompanied it when Leanne's bare foot crept up her thigh to settle insistently between her legs. Dixon looked around quickly. The table was covered by a short, checkered cloth, and anyone near them could surely see what Leanne was doing. Dixon was suddenly very grateful for the ugly plant that blocked out most of the room. An elderly couple occupied the only table with a view of Leanne's antics. Dixon prayed their eyesight wouldn't allow them to see that far.

Ralph and Alice were immersed in a conversation on Native American culture and oblivious to everything that was going on around them. Leanne was innocently eating her salad. Dixon took her napkin from her lap and wiped her lips. As she placed it back in her lap she tried to push Leanne's foot away, but Leanne wasn't ready to leave yet. With one swift move she pinned Dixon's hand against her crotch. Dixon's face burned as she realized what the elderly couple would see now if they looked up. She looked at Leanne pleadingly. A smile played across

Leanne's face as her toes pushed Dixon's fingers against her shorts. Despite her embarrassment Dixon felt herself growing aroused.

The waitress appeared beside Dixon to refill her water glass. Dixon yanked her hand from under the table so sharply she caused water to slosh out of her glass.

"Sorry," she muttered to the startled waitress. Ralph halted in midsentence.

"Are you all right?" Alice asked as the waitress left.

"Yeah, I'm fine. The waitress just surprised me," Dixon said lamely.

"Dixon, you're too nervous. You ought to find some way to release your stress," Leanne said as her toes again began to work.

Ralph and Alice shrugged, unaware of Leanne's antics. Leanne launched into a conversation about some of the artifacts they had recovered from the dig, while Dixon quietly choked down her food as the alternating pressure of Leanne's toes brought her closer and closer to the edge. Each time Dixon felt herself slipping over it, Leanne's foot would pull back and wait. Dixon almost laughed aloud from relief when Ralph finally announced he needed to get back to the motel to call Colonel Oliver.

They stepped out into the steamy, night air. A slight breeze gave some relief from the earlier humidity and kept the mosquitoes at bay. Dixon's legs trembled from the constant tension Leanne's toes had been subjecting her to for the last hour.

"Let's go for a stroll before we go back to the motel," Leanne suggested to Dixon. "I ate too much of that delicious bread and need to walk it off."

Dixon wasn't sure her legs would carry her back to the motel, much less around the town. With a wave they left Ralph and Alice and headed in the opposite direction.

"I saw a nice little park down this way when we drove in," Leanne said, and slipped her arm under Dixon's.

"Leanne, small towns aren't usually very tolerant. I'm not sure it's a good idea to be walking like this," Dixon said nervously and looked around. They appeared to be the only people in the area.

"There's no one around. If we see anyone, I promise to straighten up immediately," Leanne whispered into Dixon's ear. Dixon tried to ignore both the shiver of excitement that ran through her and the pressure of Leanne's hand against the side of her breast.

The park was small, and only one light still worked. Leanne led the way to a wooden bench deep in the shadows. "Do you feel safe back here?" Her tongue was tracing Dixon's ear.

"Why don't we just go back to the room?"

"And miss making love under the stars? Where's your sense of adventure?"

"Leanne, we're too old to be making out on park benches."

"Speak for yourself." Leanne's hand slid under Dixon's shirt and cupped her breast. "Don't try to deny it. The possibility of being caught in the restaurant turned you on."

Dixon didn't want to admit it had. "Homophobia is

rampant, and it's silly to deliberately put ourselves at risk." She tried to sound responsible, but Leanne's mouth on her breast was making it almost impossible.

Leanne unfastened Dixon's shorts and slid her hand inside. "This tells me you're a liar," Leanne whispered, dipping into Dixon's wetness as she slid to her knees and pulled Dixon's shorts down. "If you're so worried about people, why don't you keep watch while I indulge in my after-dinner dessert."

An Army battalion could have marched by and Dixon wouldn't have noticed. She was too engrossed in the long, slow rhythm of Leanne's tongue. It was well after midnight before they left the park.

The dig was drawing to a close. Dixon and Leanne had spent the past six months sneaking around making love wherever they could find a few moments of privacy. In a matter of days they would be leaving, and Leanne hadn't mentioned wishing to continue their relationship. Dixon had been trying to find a way to bring it up for several weeks, but she wasn't sure she wanted to prolong this relationship. Leanne was great in bed, but that was as far as they had got. They had never held a conversation for more than two minutes, and Leanne's idea of a serious discussion was where they would be meeting later.

They were supposed to meet in the classification tent that evening, and Dixon was determined that they would talk about their future or the lack of one.

Leanne was already waiting for her when Dixon arrived. "Come here," Leanne called as Dixon came in. "I've been missing you."

Dixon felt her resolve slip as Leanne pulled her shirt off and stepped closer to Dixon.

"We need to talk," Dixon said, forcing her eyes away from Leanne's breasts.

"I love to talk to you," Leanne whispered into Dixon's ear as she tugged Dixon's shirt from her jeans.

Dixon's shirt was off, and Leanne's bare breasts were pushing against her as she gave Dixon a kiss that scorched the soles of her feet. Dixon tried to pull away so they could talk, but Leanne's hand was in Dixon's jeans.

As Leanne's fingers slipped into her, Dixon gave up trying to talk and reached for the button on Leanne's jeans.

Dixon's knees weakened as Leanne's fingers made their way deep inside her. Without fully realizing how, she found herself lying on the tent floor. The added pressure of Leanne's thigh between her legs was more than she could handle, and she slipped over the edge into the swirling tide of pleasure.

Leanne's body stiffened, and Dixon felt the warm juices of Leanne's excitement gush over her fingers. They lay gasping for air for several seconds before Leanne's hands closed around Dixon's hips and pulled her closer.

Dixon grabbed her hands. "Wait. We have to talk."

"We just did," Leanne purred and closed her lips around Dixon's nipple.

"I mean really talk. You know, as in a conversation," Dixon persisted.

Leanne stopped and sighed. "Please tell me this isn't going to be the old what-happens-with-us-now conversation."

Dixon felt her face flush.

"Dixon," Leanne said, and stood up. She held her hand out to help Dixon up before she reached for her shirt and pulled it on. "I told you up front that I wasn't looking for a lifetime commitment." Leanne suddenly seemed very cold and far away.

Dixon pulled her clothes on. "So you're not interested in trying to maintain this relationship after we leave?" Dixon asked and tried to keep the hurt out of her voice. She knew in her heart that she wasn't interested in building anything permanent with Leanne, but the fact that Leanne had never been interested in having a committed relationship with her hurt her feelings.

Leanne ran her hand down her long braid and tossed it back over her shoulder. "I'm already in a committed relationship."

Dixon was dumbfounded.

"Don't look so offended," Leanne snapped. "I never talked about forever. I thought you understood this was just a pleasant way to help pass the time. I'm very committed to my lover."

Dixon sputtered. "How the hell can you be 'very committed' when you've been fucking me for the last six months?"

"Because that's exactly what we've been doing — fucking. I've never made love to you. I've *fucked* you!" Leanne's voice shook with anger.

Dixon swayed from the impact of the words. Tears burned her eyes as she turned to leave.

"Dixon, wait." Leanne's hand was on her arm.

"I'm sorry. I didn't mean that. You pissed me off, and I struck back. Please stay and talk to me."

Dixon glared at her.

Leanne caressed Dixon's cheek. "I'm really sorry," she apologized. "You're very special to me, but you have to be fair. I did tell you up front."

"You never told me you had a lover."

"And you never asked."

Dixon was torn between a dignified exit and hearing about why Leanne had slept with her. As usual her curiosity won. "Why didn't you tell me about her?" An awful thought struck her. "My god, it is a *her*, isn't it? Your lover, I mean."

Leanne sighed. "Of course, it's a woman. I didn't tell you because it wasn't any of your business."

Dixon started to protest, but Leanne raised her hand to stop her. "Dixon, what I have with Faye has nothing to do with what happened between you and me."

"Does she know about us?"

Leanne hesitated. "I haven't told her, but I suspect she knows. Just as I suspect that when she goes away there are others. She's a sales rep and spends a lot of time on the road." Leanne pulled a metal chair away from a table and sat down. "We don't expect each other not to sleep with other women, but we don't talk about it, either."

"How can you call that a committed relationship?"

"We both expect the other one to come home afterward," Leanne said, shrugging her shoulders. "I'm sorry if I've hurt you."

Dixon shifted uncomfortably. "I feel stupid," she admitted.

Leanne stood, walked to her, and carefully

embraced her. "You shouldn't. I've had a wonderful time, and I'll never forget you. You looked so lost the first time I saw you sitting all alone on the bus. I wanted to make you happy, and there's only one way I know how to do that." She kissed Dixon softly, but Dixon pulled away. Leanne stepped back.

"I think it would probably be best if we just spent the next few days being friends," Dixon said, knowing she couldn't make love to Leanne now that she knew there was someone else in her life.

"I understand," Leanne said. She gave Dixon's shoulder a small squeeze and left.

Dixon stood quietly for several minutes after Leanne had left. She was alone again. Suddenly she was overwhelmed with a sense of loneliness. She missed Elizabeth so deeply the pain was almost tangible. She scrubbed her hands over her face. Wallowing in memories and pain wouldn't get her anywhere. Work. That was what she needed to concentrate on. It was time to start thinking about what she would do after this assignment ended.

CHAPTER SEVEN

Two weeks later, Dixon stumbled into her apartment. It was after midnight, and she was exhausted. The trip from Missouri had been a series of delays. Due to the bus breaking down, she had missed the last direct flight of the day to San Antonio. Tired and unwilling to remain any longer than necessary, she had taken a flight routed through Houston. The plane out of Houston had turned back with engine problems, and she had ended up with a four-hour layover.

She checked on her small family of fish and

noticed that two of the guppies were missing. She knew Mrs. Jenkins would give her a full report tomorrow. Fighting her exhaustion, she took a quick shower and fell into bed, asleep almost before her head touched the pillow.

Mrs. Jenkins caught her in the hallway the next morning. Dixon invited her to breakfast, and they went to a small diner on the corner. Mrs. Jenkins gravely informed her about the demise of two of the guppies. It took Dixon a few minutes to convince her that she didn't hold her responsible. After being vindicated, Mrs. Jenkins recounted the gossip about their neighboring tenants. Dixon listened, enjoying the woman's sharp wit and often stinging tongue. After she had depleted her source of news, Mrs. Jenkins demanded to hear about Dixon's trip and asked a million questions. It was approaching lunchtime before they casually strolled back to their apartments.

Dixon settled on her sofa and began to catch up on her personal mail, which had accumulated during the last couple of weeks. Mrs. Jenkins had been sending her mail regularly until then, but had been afraid the more recent mail would not reach Dixon before she left, so it lay waiting for her. Most of it was junk mail. There was another letter from her mom, who was still trying to get her to move back home. Dixon shuddered. Ohio was a beautiful state and she loved it, but it was definitely no option for her as long as her mom lived there. Dixon mused, *I'll move to Ohio when she moves to Texas.* That seemed to be an acceptable distance between them.

There were a couple of notes from friends whom she hadn't seen in over a year. Her eyes strayed to the calendar beside her. In three days it would be exactly one year since she had crawled back through the tunnel. She hadn't forgot the promise she had made to Elizabeth to go to the fishpond at the Alamo. Should she go? Or would it just reopen the barely healed wounds? While in Missouri, she had received a letter from Jennifer thanking her for the photos and telling her she was trying to keep an open mind, but Dixon knew she was still having problems accepting the story Dixon had related to her. Dixon rested her head against the back of the sofa and stared at the ceiling. She knew she would have trouble believing such a story herself.

Three days later, at 10:55 Dixon strolled around the grounds of the Alamo feeling slightly foolish, but she had promised Elizabeth she would be here. A pinkie swear, she reminded herself, with a fond smile at the memory of their childish ritual. Dixon looked across the lush lawn around the Alamo and wondered how a place that had known such violence could seem so peaceful. Squirrels scampered about collecting the various goodies that had been dropped by both Mother Nature and the swarm of tourists who poured through daily.

At exactly 11:00, Dixon stood staring into the murky water of the aboveground fishpond. No one else was around, and she became engrossed in the gentle swaying motions of the fish.

"Soothing, aren't they?"

Dixon jumped, surprised by the voice of an elderly man beside her.

"I didn't mean to startle you," he apologized as he closely studied her. "Do you come here often?"

"No," Dixon admitted. She took in the features of the tall, slightly stooping man beside her. Despite the heat, he wore a tailored, three-piece black suit with a dazzling white shirt that looked crisp enough to cut oneself on. He had a full crop of silver-gray hair. He seemed to be waiting for her to speak. "I'm just ..." How could she explain why she was here? "Fulfilling a promise," she added meekly.

"Keeping a promise is important. It must have been an important promise," he said, continuing to probe.

"A pinkie swear," she said, smiling.

He nodded in understanding. "I'm Randolph Jackson," he said, offering his hand. It felt cool and comforting in Dixon's.

"Dixon Hayes," she returned and noticed he paled slightly.

He stared at her for several seconds. "I've waited most of my adult life to meet you, Ms. Hayes." There was a faint quiver in his voice.

Dixon stared at him puzzled. "Why?" she asked, wondering vaguely if this was some weird version of a pickup line.

He gave a quick cough and pulled himself up sharply. "That would best be explained in my office," he said, glancing around him as he reached into his jacket pocket and extracted a wallet. From it he pulled a card. "As I said, my name is Randolph Jackson. I'm an attorney. My firm has been handling a" —he hesitated — "most unusual client for eighty-odd years. To tell you the truth, I've always thought it was a hoax or the product of a disturbed mind. But enough of that for now. If I could impose upon you to show me a photo ID, please."

Dixon hesitated. He looked harmless enough. In the far recesses of her mind she already knew this had something to do with Elizabeth. With a sense of dread, Dixon removed her wallet and handed him her driver's license. She wondered if her life would ever be calm again or if that short crawl through the tunnel would haunt her forever.

"Ms. Hayes, would you please accompany me to my office? I think it would be best for us to speak there. It's only a few blocks away, if you don't mind the walk."

Lost in thought, Dixon remained silent as they walked to his office. Did this have something to do with Elizabeth? He had said something about eighty years. *That's impossible*, she scoffed to herself. Elizabeth was dead. They had buried her almost a year ago. But somehow she knew. It had to be Elizabeth.

Randolph Jackson led her into his surprisingly modern office and motioned her to a comfortable chair in front of his desk. He pushed a glass of water into her hands. Dixon hadn't realized she was shaking until some of the water splashed onto her hand.

"Ms. Hayes, perhaps it would be best to do this when you're not so upset."

"Do what?" Dixon asked, still not sure what they were doing here.

He was watching her, concerned. "I'll have my secretary make you an appointment for tomorrow."

"No!" Dixon cried frantically. "I want to know now."

"Very well." He walked around to his desk and buzzed his secretary. "Bring in the Colter file, please."

The glass slipped from Dixon's hand. She watched numbly as the water spread across the carpet.

Mr. Jackson was calling her name, and an anxious-looking young woman was standing behind him asking if she should summon a doctor.

Dixon managed to shake her head no.

"Ms. Hayes, are you sure? You don't look at all well," he insisted, a frown of concern on his face.

"I'm fine," she whispered, trying to regain her composure. "This is all such a shock."

"Would you like some more water?" he asked, retrieving her dropped glass.

"I think your carpet's already had enough," she tried to joke, but it came out sounding lame.

"The carpet will dry. Ms. Wilson, bring her a fresh glass, please."

The woman hurried away and returned with another glass of water. Dixon carefully placed it on the table beside her. The woman hesitated, still looking concerned.

"I'm fine," Dixon assured her.

With a slight smile and a nod, the woman returned to her outer office.

There was a large, metal lockbox on his desk that Dixon hadn't noticed earlier. He picked it up and placed it directly in front of him, before removing a key from his vest pocket. "As an added safety precaution, I placed the original box inside this fire-proof one after I had it removed from the vault this morning, since I had no way of knowing the value of its contents." Dixon realized he was fishing for information, but she wasn't able to help him. After he unlocked the box he sat down and faced her. "Perhaps I should explain a few things first," he said.

Dixon could only nod.

He removed a pair of glasses from his jacket pocket and perched them on the end of his nose. "The contents of this box were given to my great-great grandfather Abram Jackson. He was an attorney here in San Antonio." He picked up a file from his desk, opened it, and began to read. "The contents were given to him by a Miss Rachel Colter, along with a very large trust fund that has ensured the firm's payment throughout the years." He cleared his throat, seemingly embarrassed at the mention of money.

"When?" Dixon's voice sounded strange to her ears.

"In 1914, after the death of her sister, Elizabeth," he read from the folder. "The account was opened just prior to the onset of World War I."

His words were meant to shock her, she was sure, but she was too engrossed in the fact that Elizabeth had lived. How could that be when they had buried her? The room blurred, and Dixon forced herself to breathe deeply and concentrate on what he was saying.

He was watching her closely with dark, shrewd eyes. "Shall I continue?"

Dixon managed a nod, and he turned his attention back to the file folder.

"Abram Jackson was instructed to retain the contents until his retirement at which time he was responsible for passing them to another attorney who would receive the same instructions until May first of this year. On that date the attorney in possession of the item was to open a sealed envelope," he said, holding up a yellowed envelope for her to see, "and follow the instructions inside." He gazed at her suspiciously over the top of his glasses. "The instructions were to meet one Dixon Hayes by the fishpond at the Alamo at precisely 11:00 A.M. and turn over the contents of the box to her."

He leaned back in his chair and removed his glasses, but his gaze never left her. "Ms. Hayes, the items in this box have been held in the care of my great-great grandfather, my great-uncle, my father, and now myself. It has waited through two world wars, numerous conflicts, and man traveling to the moon." He wiped his forehead with a handkerchief. "While I know you are under no obligation whatsoever to explain it," he said, his voice revealing a quake that hadn't been there earlier, "can you please tell me how a woman who lived in 1914 could possibly know you would be standing by a *fishpond* in San Antonio, Texas, at *precisely* 11:00 A.M. today?"

She studied him. She could see his curiosity and confusion. Several seconds ticked by while she debated whether to tell him or not. "Can I assume any information I give you would be regarded as client/attorney privilege?"

"You have my word of honor. Any information you give me will go to my grave with me, madam, unless you declare otherwise."

Dixon smiled at his choice of address and wondered briefly if he was married. She should introduce him to Mrs. Jenkins. "I'm willing to tell you as much as I know, but I'm warning you in advance, you won't believe any of it."

"Nothing could surprise me more than finding you there today," he assured her.

Dixon started her story from the point at which she and Elizabeth entered the tunnel and stopped with the discovery of Elizabeth's body and her belief that Elizabeth had been killed. She omitted little except for the true relationship between Elizabeth and Rachel.

He stared at her, unprepared to accept this explanation. "I remember reading about the death of Ms. Colter, of course," he said, shaking his head. Abruptly, he stood and reached into the lockbox, struggling to remove the contents. The wooden box he removed was fastened with several nails and two wide metal bands. "As you can see, the box was securely sealed, and I can assure you no one has ever tampered with it. It is yours now. I warn you it is rather heavy, though."

Dixon could only stare at the box as he set it on the desk in front of her.

When she didn't move, he waved toward the box. "I can make my conference room available if you'd like to open it in private."

She knew he was praying she'd open the box in front of him, but the contents were too private for her to share with anyone. "No. I'll take it with me," she said. "I'd prefer to open it alone." She sensed his disappointment.

"Very well. If I could just get you to sign some papers releasing the firm of all responsibilities for the item."

She signed several papers before standing. "Are there any financial considerations that need to be taken care of?" she asked.

"No, no. The trust fund Ms. Colter arranged has

been more than adequate. In fact, the remainder of the fund will now be turned over to her descendants."

"Descendants!" She gripped the corner of the desk for support. Of course, there could be descendants. Elizabeth had been pregnant.

He was watching her closely. "Yes," he answered and held up his hand, "but please understand, I cannot release any names to you."

"How much do they know about this?" she asked, pointing to the box.

He shrugged. "I have no way of knowing what has been handed down through family members. Judging from what was said when I've spoken to them over the years, and that was very few times indeed," he assured her quickly, "I'd have to guess that they know very little." He folded his hands on his desk. "Due to a recent death in the family, I have had to work with a new client."

"So they don't know anything about me?" Dixon asked.

"Not through the firm. But as I said, I can't be sure what they may have learned from other family members. Our position has always been that the firm was retained by Ms. Rachel Colter to hold a certain item for an undisclosed person until today's date." He shrugged and leaned back into his chair before continuing. "I called them recently to inform them of the letter that gave me instructions on how and when to locate this undisclosed person, but I told them nothing of your name or the location where we were to meet. I will now inform them that the package has been delivered and that our services are concluded."

Dixon felt a strange mixture of relief and sadness. "Of course, I understand," she said, rising to leave.

He stood quickly. "If you're ready, my secretary will drive you to your car."

"Thank you and your family for taking care of this," she said, and held out her hand. He clasped her hand in both of his.

"Rachel Colter has been the firm's most interesting client for many years," he confided with a smile.

Dixon patted the heavy box before picking it up. "I'm sure Elizabeth would have been pleased with the way you've handled everything." From the look in his eyes, she could tell he still had doubts about her explanation.

The box sat on Dixon's dining room table. She found herself tiptoeing around it as though a sudden noise or movement might cause it to explode.

That night she lay in bed thinking about it, unable to open it and unable to forget it. Was it from Elizabeth or was it some sick joke? Jennifer was the only person who knew about Rachel. Could she be the source of the box?

"No! That's ridiculous," she groaned, flopping over in bed for what felt like the hundredth time. She watched the blazing red numerals on her digital clock and wrestled with her demons until 3:00 A.M. when she suddenly couldn't wait to get the box open. She had to know what was in it. It took her almost an hour to loosen the nails and twist through the metal bands that sealed it. An envelope yellowed with age lay on top. Dixon removed it, and below were three bundles of rags. She carefully opened the envelope. Tears scorched her eyes as she recognized a slightly shakier version of Elizabeth's neat, precise penmanship.

Dear Dixon,   December 23, 1913

By the time you read this I'll be long gone, but I wanted so much to share with you my experiences. Today is my 89th birthday, and since I'm not sure how many more I'll be around to see, I thought it best if I get my affairs in order now. Enclosed with this letter you should find your camera that you left behind. (You left it empty. Rachel and I have been all over the world, and we couldn't find any 35mm film. Can you imagine!) I remembered your love for collecting coins, so I've tried to save you a decent sampling of those I've come in contact with, and finally my journals. I know I can depend on you to protect them until they can be placed with the appropriate archive. I was always harping to you about women's studies and how there were so few memoirs. Well, here is my firsthand account for you. Do with them as you see fit.

Dixon, you can't begin to imagine the splendor of my life with Rachel. She's still a spry eighty-one and sends her love to you. We have traveled the world and are quite comfortable. I seem to have this knack for knowing when to buy and sell certain stocks. I'm certainly glad I majored in history! I want you to know that other than missing you and Jennifer, I have never had a single regret about staying. I hope my disappearance didn't cause you or Jennifer too much pain.

Also enclosed is a photo of Dixon Junior, our darling daughter. I have always told her stories about your daring adventures and exploits, in the form of fairy tales, of course. She does have your charming personality.

Dixon's hands flew through the box until she found the stack of small, faded pictures. One was a studio shot of Elizabeth, Rachel, and a small baby. Elizabeth and Rachel were similarly dressed and Dixon laughed through her tears trying to imagine her dear friend adapting to hoopskirts, bustles, and the other fashions that would have confronted her. There were three other pictures of Dixon Junior. One when she looked about five, one around fourteen, and a wedding picture where she stood with a dapper-looking young man. Dixon turned back to the letter.

She has been the joy of our lives. My journal entries will allow you to share her growing up.

My greatest fear in life has been that I will do something that will drastically alter history. There were some sorely tempting times in my life to interfere, but to date I have managed to mind my own business. The history books we grew up with failed miserably to correctly portray the misery and horror that the Civil War inflicted upon all regions of this nation. Rachel, Dixon, and I went to England to avoid it. I couldn't in good conscience stand by and watch the devastation and death. It is 1913, and the world is on the brink of another horrendous phase. I have prepared Rachel for what is coming. If I am not here she will know what to do to protect our small family from the disasters that are about to occur. I have also tried to prepare Dixon Junior, without giving her any specifics. As you can see, I'm still a worrywart. It is so hard to stand by and know what's coming, but again my journals will convey that.

The day you left I had a most unusual experience after I freed you and was safety back on my side of the tunnel. I peered through to make certain you had made it safely, and I saw myself crawling behind you. I must say it was a rather eerie feeling. I have often wondered if I'm still living there with you; if so, then this correspondence will certainly come as a great shock to you and my twentieth-century self as well, I suppose. Perhaps I exist in both dimensions.

I will entrust this package into the care of my descendants and hope they carry forth my wishes. I can only hope I will still have descendants and that they have not already vanished into the dust of history.

My darling Dixon, your life is just beginning. It will speed by so quickly, so enjoy it to the fullest, but you always did, my brave and adventurous friend.

Love, your friend through the ages,
Elizabeth "Pinkie Swear"

Dixon cradled her head on the table and cried until there were no more tears. Her tears were a celebration for the lives of Elizabeth, Rachel, and Dixon Junior and their happiness. For the briefest instant Dixon regretted her decision to return through the tunnel, but she knew she would not have been happy living during that violent and oppressive era.

When her tears finally stopped, she finished going through the contents of the box. There was a large bag of coins. She smiled as she set them aside for later. Elizabeth had never understood her hobby of coin collecting. Paying money for money doesn't make sense, she would argue, but she had spent her life collecting them for Dixon and had sent them to her through time.

In another bundle of cloth she found her camera. The chrome plating had darkened with age, and the shutter release was stuck. Six large leather-bound journals lay in the bottom of the box. She pulled one out and hugged it tightly to her. She imagined she could smell Elizabeth's scent on it. She checked the dates of each journal and carefully stacked them in chronological sequence. Taking the top one, she began to read.

It took her a week and a half to finish the journals. Many entries she read over and over until she felt she had lived the experience with Elizabeth. As she closed the last journal, Dixon felt released from the final shreds of pain at losing Elizabeth. She laughed aloud at the sheer joy of being alive. After a long, hot shower, she sat down and telephoned old friends. She made lunch dates, dinner dates, and vowed never again to withdraw from life. Elizabeth's journals had shown her how full and valuable life could be.

For the next month, Dixon was a whirlwind of

activity. She vaguely realized that she had swung from one extreme to the other, but she had to get it out of her system before she could find a balance. The only thing she still avoided was her love life. There just didn't seem to be anyone who caught her attention.

She even shocked her friends by attending the Lesbians in Government fund-raising dance. Dixon went alone and had a great time. She ran into women she hadn't seen in ages and laughed and danced with old friends and a few unknown women who approached her. While there she made plans with her long-neglected friends Gloria and Teresa to attend a concert at the Sunken Gardens Theater the following weekend. Dixon stayed at the dance until the final song, which was traditionally a slow number, intended for lovers or those who soon would be. As the beginning notes sounded, she slipped away.

Dixon was on her way out the door to the concert at the Sunken Gardens Theater when her phone rang. Glancing at her watch, she groaned. She was already late, but it might be Gloria and Teresa canceling. She grabbed the phone. "Hello."

"Ms. Hayes?"

"Yes."

"This is Randolph Jackson. I have a matter to discuss with you. Are you free for a few minutes?"

"Actually, I was on my way out the door, Mr. Jackson."

"It'll only take a moment," he assured her.

Dixon sighed and sat on the sofa. She was already late. A few more minutes wouldn't make much difference. "What can I do for you?"

"A descendant of Ms. Colter's has contacted me

several times wanting to meet you. She has been so insistent that I finally told her I would contact you and let you decide."

"No!" Dixon's heart pounded. "Under no circumstances do I want to see anyone claiming to be a descendant of Elizabeth Colter!" She slammed the phone down and raced out the door. She drove aimlessly, the concert forgotten. She tried to determine why she had reacted so violently to his phone call. After hours of unanswered questions, she returned to her apartment and dialed Jennifer's number. John, her husband, answered.

"John, Dixon Hayes. Is Jennifer in?"

"Yeah, hold on. I'll get her for you."

A moment later Jennifer's voice sounded in her ear.

"Jennifer, can you come to my apartment?"

There was a slight pause. "Now?"

"Yes."

"Dixon, it's almost midnight."

Dixon glanced stupidly at her watch. "I'm sorry," she mumbled. "I lost track of time."

"Are you all right? I can be there in twenty minutes if this is an emergency. Are you sick?"

"No. I'm sorry. I didn't realize it was so late."

"What's going on?" When Dixon didn't respond, she added, "Dixon, talk to me."

"It's about Elizabeth."

"What about her?" Jennifer asked cautiously.

"She didn't die. She had the baby, and now a descendant of hers wants to talk to me."

Jennifer was quiet for so long that Dixon was beginning to wonder if she had hung up.

"I think you should consider talking to a psychologist," Jennifer said evenly. "Elizabeth's death has been hard on you, and with the anniversary of it having rolled around, you're being subjected to the same emotions again. Let me make an appointment with a friend of mine. I know she can help you. She has helped me a lot."

Dixon hung up the phone and turned it off. She sat staring into space for several minutes. She wasn't losing her mind. She just needed someone who would believe her and help her deal with the news that Elizabeth had a descendant who was looking for her. She went into the bedroom and got the pictures of Elizabeth, Rachel, and Dixon Junior and returned to the living room. Curling up on the sofa, she stared at the face of her dear friend.

"Would you want me to meet this woman?" she asked the image in the photo. No answer came as she sat staring at the photos.

The doorbell rang, but Dixon ignored it. She was certain it was Mrs. Jenkins, and she wasn't up to talking to her. It rang again, followed by a sharp knock and Jennifer calling out.

"Dixon, it's me, Jennifer. Open the door."

Dixon trudged to the door and unlocked it. Jennifer flew in so quickly she almost knocked Dixon over. Tears were streaming down her face.

"Dixon, I love Elizabeth too. I miss her and want her back in my life. I know you're hurting, but you've got to stop this obsession with this . . . this other time dimension business. Elizabeth died in the landslide. We buried her body. She's gone."

Dixon handed the photo of Elizabeth, Rachel, and

Dixon Junior to her. Jennifer snatched it away to look at it. Dixon caught her as she swayed, and led her to the sofa. Jennifer continued to stare at the photo for several minutes. "This is some kind of sick joke. What's going on?" Her eyes seemed large and lost in her pale face.

Dixon told her about the promise she had made to Elizabeth at the tunnel. Then she told her about her meeting with Randolph Jackson. She showed Jennifer the other photos that had been in the box and then gave her Elizabeth's letter. While Jennifer read through the letter, Dixon stacked Elizabeth's journals on the table before them.

"Those are her journals," Dixon said when Jennifer laid the letter down.

Jennifer picked up the top one and read the first entry. "I need to call John to let him know I won't be home for a while," she said, dazed.

Dixon turned the phone on and left to make a pot of coffee.

When she returned to the living room with the coffee, she curled up on the opposite end of the sofa as Jennifer began to read.

Jennifer talking on the phone woke her the next morning; Dixon had fallen asleep on the sofa. She carefully stretched her stiff muscles and gazed at the sunshine pouring in the window.

Jennifer hung up the phone and turned to her. "I canceled my appointments for the day. I think we should talk."

"You don't still think I'm crazy, do you?" Dixon asked defensively.

"I'm afraid we both may be," she replied and sat on the sofa facing Dixon. She looked lost, and Dixon's heart went out to her. During the past year Jennifer's hair had grown much grayer, and wrinkles now creased her once-smooth forehead.

Jennifer suddenly struck her knees with her fists. "This is impossible. I saw her body!" Fresh tears were streaming down her cheeks. "Elizabeth did die."

Dixon slid over and took her hand. "I've had longer to think about this, and I think that in a way Elizabeth is dead."

"I *know* she's dead!" Jennifer shouted. "I identified the body, remember?"

"Maybe what you saw was . . ." Dixon jumped up, frustrated. "I don't have a vocabulary for this." She stopped in front of her. "I think they found Elizabeth's body because she had already lived her life here. I think the twentieth-century Elizabeth died the day we crawled through the tunnel, and this allowed her to continue living in this other time."

Jennifer held up her hands to stop her. "Dixon, please try to understand this from my point of view. I'm a doctor. I know exactly how life starts, how it continues, and how it stops. One part of me is screaming this whole story is an elaborate, sick hoax, while another part of me knows without a doubt that Elizabeth wrote those journals." She pointed to the journal she had read. "This is destroying the basic premise of life as I know it. I don't want to know that my baby sister's great-great granddaughter is out there walking around."

"So you don't want to meet her?"

"No!"

"Are you sure?"

Jennifer picked up the photo of Elizabeth, Rachel, and Dixon Junior and stared at it. "No, I'm not sure, but I know I'm not ready now. I may never be." She took a deep quivering breath before placing the picture back on the table. "Elizabeth would hate me for what I'm about to do, but this continuance is killing me. I have to get over Elizabeth's death in my own way. Whether she lived a hundred years ago or not is irrelevant. I've still lost her." She looked at Dixon. "I need time. I'd appreciate it if you didn't contact me again. Maybe someday I can learn to cope with this, but for now I have to believe Elizabeth died a year ago." She rushed to the door. "I'm sorry," she called over her shoulder as the door closed behind her.

Dixon looked at her watch. It was a little after 8:00. She showered and walked to the corner diner for breakfast. *Jennifer is wrong*, she mused over her scrambled eggs and toast. Elizabeth had not died in the landslide. She had died in 1914, and somewhere out there was a part of her wanting to find its way back to Dixon.

Dixon phoned Randolph Jackson from the diner and asked him to make arrangements for Elizabeth's descendant to meet her.

"Where and when would be convenient for you?" he asked.

"Eleven, Saturday morning at the fishpond by the Alamo," she answered without thinking.

"Of course," he sighed. "I'll let you know as soon as possible."

Dixon had another cup of coffee before making her way home. The light was blinking on her answering machine when she came in. She pushed the button and listened to Randolph Jackson's voice. "Ms. Hayes, your meeting has been scheduled as you requested. The woman with whom you are to meet does not wish to reveal her name at this point; therefore, I felt it only fair not to reveal yours to her. She will be wearing a white jacket with a red carnation and jeans. Please don't hesitate to call me if I can be of further assistance."

Somehow Dixon doubted he truly meant that. She spent the day cleaning her camera equipment and preparing for an upcoming shoot she had for a local architectural firm. The phone interrupted her. It was Gloria.

"Sorry about the concert last night," Dixon said before Gloria could scold her. "Something came up at the last minute, and it was too late to call you. Did you and Teresa have a good time?"

"Yeah, it was pretty good. Listen, I'm calling to see what you're doing tonight. I know it's short notice, but we'd like for you to come over to the house for dinner."

"Actually, I was planning on working."

"I could've hit you with the guilt approach, since the concert was your idea," Gloria said.

"All right," Dixon said smiling. "What time? You know I can't handle guilt."

"Is 7:00 okay with you?"

"That's fine."

"Good. I gotta go. My other line's ringing. Listen, dress up a little, will you? We may go out afterward. Later."

Dixon stood holding the dead phone. Gloria was an investment counselor, and time was money.

CHAPTER EIGHT

Dixon arrived precisely at 7:00. She had on her best navy blazer and silk pants. Gloria, a wiry blond with a wicked sense of humor, opened the door for her.

"Am I presentable?" Dixon asked, stepping into the spacious Victorian-style home. "The only suit I have that looks better than this is my birthday suit," she teased, giving Gloria a quick hug. Dixon turned and came face to face with a tall brunet wearing black tailored slacks and a pale-cream shirt with its sleeves rolled to mid-forearm. Her feet were encased in soft black leather boots that sported a tiny gold chain draped across each top. "Shit," Dixon uttered, gazing into warm pools of liquid gold.

"Dixon Hayes, meet Megan Bishop." Gloria's lean frame slid past Dixon. "You two get acquainted. I have to see if Teresa needs any help in the kitchen." Gloria was gone before either could protest.

Megan extended her hand. "Were you told to make yourself presentable?" she asked in a voice that poured over Dixon like fresh honey.

"As a matter of fact, I was," Dixon replied, sounding much calmer than she felt as she continued to cling to Megan's hand.

"It makes you wonder what they think we look like the rest of the time," Megan said and gave a warm smile. "We may as well sit down. They'll probably leave us out here alone forever."

Dixon released her hand with a great deal of reluctance. "Do you think we're being officially fixed up?" Dixon asked, suddenly very grateful to Gloria and Teresa.

"I do believe so. Shall we get even?" There was a mischievous twinkle in her eyes that Dixon was drawn to.

"What have you got in mind?"

"Let's sneak out. It'll be twenty minutes before they even miss us."

"That's kind of mean, isn't it? Think of the leftovers they'll have."

"I am," Megan answered with a grin.

"Let's go."

They slipped out the door and raced down the sidewalk to Dixon's car like two wayward kids.

"I'm parked across the street." Megan nodded toward a small Ford. "Do you like Italian food?"

"Love it."

"Then follow me. I know one of the best places in town."

They drove to the far south side of town. The place was small but warm with atmosphere and smelled delicious. They sat across from each other and waited for the waitress to finish taking their order.

"I've always considered Dixon an unusual name," Megan said, sipping her wine. "My grandfather's name was Mason Dixon O'Conner. I guess it's more common than I assumed."

"His parents must have been truly angry when he was born," Dixon teased.

Megan released her incredible laugh again, and Dixon realized she was grinning like a fool. But she couldn't seem to stop.

"What do you do?" Dixon managed to ask while playing with her wineglass.

"I'm a pilot."

"Commercial or private?"

"Private. Helicopter. I own a charter service. I recently moved to Texas from California," Megan said.

"What brought you back?"

"My dad died and I came out to settle his affairs. Once I was back, I remembered how much I love the area and decided to move my business here."

Dixon saw a flash of sadness in Megan's eyes and yearned to remove it.

"I'm sorry for your loss," she muttered, knowing it did little to help. "Why did you leave originally, if you loved it so much?" Dixon persisted.

Megan shrugged. "Silly reasons. I thought I could run away from —" She stopped sharply. "What about you?" she asked, changing the subject.

"I'm a freelance photographer." Dixon noticed the sudden shift in conversation but decided to ignore it. People ran from all kinds of things. Most of the reasons were completely harmless and often seemed silly to someone else.

"Sounds interesting. What have you done recently?"

Dixon launched into a recap of her trip to Missouri, careful to omit any reference to her encounters with Leanne in her narrative.

As Megan had promised the food was great, and they laughed and lingered over it until the staff began their not-too-discreet closing preparations.

"It looks like they're ready to close," Megan said.

Dixon looked around, startled to see that they were the only customers left.

"I think you're right," she agreed. They paid their bill and strolled to their cars.

"I enjoyed tonight," Dixon replied when they reached her car. The night air was too warm, and Dixon slipped off her jacket and tossed it onto the backseat of her car.

"Me, too," Megan agreed. An awkward silence fell between them.

"I'd like to see you again," Dixon said.

"Would tomorrow be too soon?" Megan asked, staring at her boldly. "If you're free I could take you up in a helicopter. I have an early run to Corpus, but I'm free after that. There's nothing like flying over the water in a helicopter. Unless you don't like to fly."

Dixon heard the soft challenge. "I love to fly."

"Great. I'll see you at 8:00 at this address." She pulled a business card from her pocket.

Dixon took the card and placed it in her shirt pocket.

"Can I have your home number?" Megan asked.

Dixon retrieved her wallet and handed Megan one of her cards. "What would we do without business cards?" she asked as Megan's fingers brushed against hers.

"I'll see you tomorrow," Megan said, stepping forward and lightly kissing Dixon on the lips. She was gone before Dixon could react.

Dixon drove home in a soft daze, still feeling the warm texture of Megan's lips against hers. She had two messages from Gloria and Teresa on the machine. She called them. Teresa answered on the first ring.

"Where did you two go?" she demanded.

"Teresa, we couldn't help ourselves." Dixon heard Gloria pick up the extension. "We fell so head-over-heels in love, we weren't able to keep our hands off of each other." Dixon couldn't resist one final jab. "You two are such dear friends to set us up like that and then run off and leave us alone."

"Damn, did you two rehearse that or what?" Gloria groaned.

"Why?"

"Because it's almost word for word what Megan said when she called," Teresa said and laughed.

Dixon joined the laughter and promised to make up the night to them later. She was crawling into bed when Megan called. "I wanted to thank you for the wonderful evening," she said, her smooth voice caressing Dixon's ear.

"I had a great time," Dixon said, as she stretched

out on the bed and tried to ignore the warm glow that was building between her legs.

"I'll see you in the morning."

Dixon, feeling like a teenager with her first crush, held the phone for several seconds after Megan hung up.

Dixon arrived at Bishop's Air Transport Service a half hour early. She made herself drive around until 7:45. With a deep breath to steady her nerves, she hung her camera around her neck and grabbed her gear bag. The day was already warm, and she was glad she had worn the sleeveless denim shirt and a pair of shorts. Wanting everything to be perfect, she had agonized over what to wear.

Megan was on the phone in a tiny office that was surprisingly neat and homey. Dixon realized she had anticipated finding a room filled with grease-stained rags and flight logs. Megan flashed a smile that made Dixon feel as though she had just been given a great reward. She motioned for Dixon to sit on the couch across from her, but Dixon was too nervous and wandered around trying to appear calm until Megan finished her phone conversation.

"Are you ready?" Megan asked. She gave Dixon a hug that sent Dixon's stomach plunging. The camera around her neck was an unwanted barrier between them.

"Yeah," she managed to croak out.

"You're not afraid of flying, are you?" Megan asked, apparently mistaking Dixon's nervousness for preflight jitters.

"No. I love to fly."

"Great. Let's go." They walked through the building. Megan was wearing a pair of white denim shorts that heightened the richness of her tanned legs. Dixon was so absorbed in watching the enticing ripple of the muscles in her calves that she nearly ran over her when Megan stopped to open the door. Four helicopters perched like giant dragonflies on a large open area in the back.

"You own all of this?" Dixon asked, wondering what a helicopter cost.

"Well, the bank and I own this," Megan said, waving at the area. "Hop in, and I'll make sure you're secure."

Dixon stepped up into the open cockpit and settled in the seat. Megan retrieved a seat belt and draped herself across Dixon to fasten it. "Don't want you falling out," she said, her face only inches from Dixon's. The belt snapped shut, and Megan causally gripped Dixon's bare thigh just above her knee. "That should do it," she said and smiled, tightening her grip for a moment.

Dixon's heart was tap-dancing in her chest.

Megan pulled a headset from somewhere above Dixon's head and gently placed it on Dixon. She casually stroked the hair back from each side of Dixon's face. Her warm hands seemed to linger longer than necessary. Her fingertips gently brushed Dixon's jaw. She stepped away only to appear a moment later crawling into the pilot's seat. She fastened her seat belt and began to flip switches. The rotor blades began a slow steady swirl, gradually increasing in speed until they violently churned the air around them.

Megan slipped on a headset, and her voice flowed

into Dixon's ears. Dixon clung to the seat to keep herself from grabbing Megan and kissing her. Megan saw the gesture and misinterpreted it. She closed a soft hand over Dixon's clenched one. "Don't be scared," she whispered. "I'll take good care of you." Dixon felt her desire soak her shorts as she forced herself to concentrate on the city spreading out below them. The helicopter continued to rise, and Dixon began to snap pictures.

"I hope you have plenty of film, because you're going to love flying over the Gulf," Megan promised.

Dixon watched in amazement as Megan set the helicopter down on the roof of the building with no more fuss than Dixon used in loading a roll of film. "I'll only be a few minutes," Megan called to her. "Will you be okay?"

"I'm fine," Dixon assured her, and gave her brightest smile to reinforce it. A warm flush spread across Megan's cheeks, and Dixon saw the slight parting of her lips. Without another word, Megan hopped out, grabbed a small package from behind her seat, and was gone.

Dixon leaned her head back and closed her eyes. The excitement from last night's dinner and the anticipation of what today might hold had kept her awake most of the night. It had been a long time since she had felt this way about anyone. Leanne had been nice, but Leanne had been about sex. She tried to ignore the mounting pressure building between her legs. Part of this was definitely about sex, too, she chided herself, but with Megan she sensed there was more. *I've got to think of something else.* She began chanting her ABC's backward.

A warm hand stroked her thigh. Dixon gasped as she shot forward. "I didn't mean to frighten you," Megan's voice came through the headset. Her hand was still on Dixon's thigh.

"I must have dozed," Dixon stammered, trying to control the various parts of her body that had suddenly developed wills of their own.

"Well, hang on, because I'm about to wake you up."

If you wake me up any more . . .

Twenty minutes later, Dixon was lost in a world of total sensory awareness as the helicopter swooped over the Texas Gulf Coast waters. She became so mesmerized that she forgot about her camera until a school of dolphins came into view and her years of training kicked in. Only the seat belt kept her from falling as she leaned out to capture the antics of the playful creatures. She was vaguely aware of Megan's laughter and turned the camera on her.

Megan set the helicopter down on a stretch of deserted beach. "I'm starving," Megan said, stripping off her headset.

Dixon was surprised to discover that she too was famished. She glanced at her watch; it was well past lunchtime. "Are we ordering out?" she asked, staring up and down the deserted beach.

"No, we have O'Conner takeout," Megan teased and lifted a large picnic basket from behind Dixon. "Grab the blanket that's back there," she called over her shoulder.

They spread the blanket in the shade of the helicopter. The warm spring weather was perfect. Megan opened a chilled thermos. "We have roast beef sandwiches, potato chips, and various goodies." She pulled out a plastic bowl and handed Dixon an assortment of olives and pickles. "To drink we have iced tea." She held up a large beverage thermos and plastic glasses.

"You've thought of everything, haven't you?" Dixon asked, biting into a sandwich.

"I certainly hope so," she said and gave Dixon a heart-stopping look.

Dixon managed to choke down the sandwich while Megan told her about various flights she had made. Dixon was sure they were interesting stories, but she kept losing her train of thought as she watched Megan's perfect mouth form the words.

"Let's go for a walk," Megan suggested after they finished eating. She offered her hand to help Dixon up. Dixon didn't let go of it as they strolled down the beach. They walked, making only a few quiet comments on the beauty of the water. After several minutes, they turned and started back to the helicopter. They silently packed the picnic items and returned them to the helicopter. Dixon reached for the blanket.

"Why don't you leave that?" Megan was beside her, running her hand down Dixon's back. "We may find another use for it."

Dixon turned to face her as Megan's hands tugged Dixon's shirt from her shorts and let her fingertips caress Dixon's sides.

"I wanted to do this last night," Megan's throaty voice whispered against Dixon's ear.

"You should have," Dixon whispered back as her own hands slid up Megan's thighs.

Megan's lips lightly brushed Dixon's cheek before tracing the contour of her ear. A moan escaped Dixon as Megan's tongue delicately swept along her jawbone. Her lips fluttered across Dixon's trembling lips. Dixon swayed toward her, but Megan pulled back. "No, don't move."

Her lips again began their exploration of Dixon's face and neck. She nipped Dixon's shoulder lightly, causing Dixon to beg, "Megan, please, let me touch you."

"Not yet." As her fingers deftly unbuttoned Dixon's shirt, her lips trailed behind them, scorching Dixon's skin. The shirt was pushed away, and Megan's lips moved back up Dixon's shoulder to her neck. Dixon's bra straps were pushed from her shoulders, and Megan's lips slid down to rest between Dixon's breasts. Megan pulled the cloth barrier away and released the hooks at the same time. Her tongue teased Dixon's aching nipples.

Unable to stop herself, Dixon's hands flew to Megan's head, but Megan grabbed them and held them away from her as her lips continued their journey down Dixon's stomach.

"Stand still," Megan commanded. "You're too impatient." Her eyes darkened to a burnished gold. She released Dixon's hands and began to unbutton Dixon's shorts, one slow button at a time.

Dixon strained to stand still as Megan's fingers

brushed against her abdomen with each released button. The last button gave way, and Dixon's shorts slipped down her legs. Megan pushed down Dixon's underwear.

Dixon's breath caught in a sharp intake as the warm Gulf breeze blew against her naked skin. She gritted her teeth and forced herself to remain still.

Megan's eyes twinkled as she leaned into her. "That's much better." Megan's lips closed around Dixon's nipple, and her hands dropped to Dixon's hips. Dixon locked her hands behind her head to keep from grabbing Megan. Never had she wanted to touch someone so badly in her life. Megan's lips were exploring Dixon's stomach as her hands trailed up and down Dixon's back, her short nails softly scratching. Her hands worked their way down to Dixon's crumpled shorts and underwear, and encouraged Dixon to step out of them.

Megan's tongue brushed through the tangled patch between Dixon's legs, and Dixon began to tremble. Megan helped her lie down on the blanket.

Dixon opened her eyes to find Megan leaning over her. "I have to touch you," Dixon rasped. "Please."

Megan sat up and removed her shirt. Dixon watched as Megan unfastened her bra to reveal the generous, creamy breasts, the nipples dark and swollen. She stood, removed her shorts, and dropped them into a heap near Dixon's. She placed a foot on either side of Dixon's waist and looked down at her.

"Then touch me," Megan breathed.

Dixon's hands tentatively reached for Megan's tight calves as Megan glided to her knees. She leaned forward and gazed into Dixon's eyes. Slowly their lips met. The liquid fire flowing through her veins overwhelmed Dixon. Megan's hand closed over Dixon's breast, teasing the nipple with her fingertips as Dixon's body arched upward.

Dixon's hand slipped down Megan's back until it trailed through the slippery wetness of Megan's desire. Megan suddenly shifted and stretched out alongside her. Dixon became lost in the exquisite feel of Megan's lips and hands claiming her body, and the feel of Megan's body against her own hands and lips. A loud moan escaped Dixon as Megan captured a swollen nipple and pulled it lightly between her teeth. Megan's fingers leisurely parted Dixon's swollen lips and stroked the velvety softness. She continued the subtle rhythm until Dixon's body tensed and rocked against her as the spasms of pleasure shook her.

Dixon grasped Megan's shoulders and rolled her onto her back. In frantic desperation she encircled Megan's dark swollen nipples with her tongue, alternating between them until Megan begged for release. Dixon's mouth made its way down Megan's stomach, her tongue drifting across the dampness of Megan's desire and each stroke becoming gradually longer and deeper until she plunged her tongue into the creamy center. Megan's hips rose from the blanket as her hands clutched Dixon's head. Dixon drank deeply until Megan's hoarse cry cut through the breaking waves of the Gulf waters.

Their lovemaking slowed to a sensual exploration and continued through the afternoon until they fell into an exhausted slumber. On the flight back to San Antonio they talked. Megan talked about her business and her worries of its not prospering or of its prospering so much it would become unmanageable. Dixon spoke of her dream of that one perfect photo.

The sun had long since set before they returned to San Antonio.

The rotor blades wound down to a slow whirl as Dixon released her seat belt and leaned across to kiss Megan. She wanted to spend the night with her, but tomorrow was the day she was to meet Elizabeth's mysterious descendant, and she needed time to prepare herself emotionally for the encounter.

"I'd love to spend the night with you, but I have an early commitment," she said as she smoothed a lock of Megan's hair from her forehead.

"Can I see you tomorrow night? I could cook dinner and then we could . . ." Megan let the sentence drift off as her hand trailed up Dixon's thigh.

Dixon felt the slow burn begin in her stomach and ooze down into her groin. "This is not the place to start something," she murmured as her hands slipped beneath Megan's shirt and began to caress her breast.

Meagan leaned into her and kissed her deeply. "There's a very comfortable couch in my office," she said, pulling away. "If you don't need to rush off."

"Have you had a lot of occasions to test the comfort of this particular couch?" Dixon asked with arched brows.

"At least twice a week," Megan said, and laughed as the security lights reflected the look of shock on Dixon's face. "I tend to be a workaholic, unless I have something to distract me. Sometimes I work too late and spend the night here," Megan explained, her hand still busy making small patterns on Dixon's thigh.

"Maybe I can help you think of a distraction from all that work," Dixon offered.

They swiftly made their way into the hangar and

into Megan's office. Megan turned and pinned Dixon to the office door as soon as it closed. In one smooth move, Megan pulled off Dixon's shirt and tossed it aside.

The phone's shrill jangle jarred Dixon from sleep. Hoping it was Megan, she grabbed it and cooed good morning.

"It certainly is," Gloria's teasing voice cooed back. "Although I'm assuming that seductive greeting wasn't meant for me."

Laughing, Dixon fell back onto her bed. The clock on the nightstand read 7:23. "To what do I owe this wake-up call?" she asked.

"Your favorite nosy friends are interested in your love life. I have instructions to get complete details or else Teresa will be over tonight to extract them from you through those strange analytical powers of hers."

Dixon stretched lazily and smiled, thinking of Teresa's soft, patient voice and caring eyes that made a person want to tell her things one would never tell anyone else.

"That's why she's such a great psychologist," Dixon said. "As for my love life" — she hesitated and felt her body respond as she recalled making love to Megan on the beach and later in her office — "let's just say it seems to have been reborn."

"It's about time," Gloria replied happily. "We were beginning to wonder if you were cloistered."

"Thanks for introducing me to Megan."

"Hey, thank Megan. She's been after us to introduce her to you for two weeks. She was so anxious to meet you, we even brought her to the concert, but you failed to show."

Dixon blinked and sat up. "Megan wanted to meet me? How did she know me?"

"No idea, sweetie, but my other lines are starting to look like Christmas. Talk to you later."

"Wait a minute!" Dixon called, but was again talking to a dead phone. Why would Megan want to meet her? How had Megan even known about her? Dixon was certain she would have remembered Megan had they ever met before. Her alarm clock suddenly came to life. She had set it for 7:30. Time to start preparing to meet Elizabeth's descendant. She would have to save her questions until tonight.

Dixon took a long, hot shower and alternately found herself apprehensive about today's meeting and aroused at thinking about Megan.

She called Mrs. Jenkins and invited her to breakfast. She needed the distraction that her neighbor would be sure to provide.

True to form, Mrs. Jenkins kept Dixon at least partially occupied for over an hour and a half. When they returned to the apartment complex, she helped Mrs. Jenkins move a new chair that the store had delivered the day before.

"It just didn't look right where they put it," Mrs. Jenkins insisted as Dixon moved the chair closer to the window. Dixon smiled to herself. Mrs. Jenkins would now have an unobstructed view of the front entrance from her window. No one would ever again sneak in or out without her knowledge.

By the time Dixon returned to her apartment, it was almost time to leave for the Alamo. She sat on the sofa and took several deep breaths, trying to calm her escalating tension, but she couldn't sit still. She picked up her keys with a nagging feeling that she was making a terrible mistake.

CHAPTER NINE

By the time Dixon parked her car two blocks away and walked to the Alamo, the sun was already letting itself be known. She was surprised to find several more people on the Alamo grounds on this Saturday morning than there had been when she was there during the week. *It's tourist season*, she suddenly realized. Traffic would double, and so would downtown hotel and restaurant prices.

Watching the swarms of people, Dixon experienced a stab of panic. How would she and Elizabeth's descendant identify each other? Then she remembered the woman would be wearing a white jacket with a red carnation. She relaxed some. There wouldn't be many jackets, white or otherwise, in this heat. She was early and had almost a half hour to kill. On impulse she walked into the cool, dim interior of the Alamo. She stood to the side to let her eyes adjust from the bright sunlight.

She tried to absorb the wide range of accents and languages from the whispered conversations around her. She found it ironic that people would travel from all over the world to visit something that most natives of the city hadn't been to in years, if ever.

When her eyes had adjusted to the dim lighting, she walked deeper into the shrine where a tall, attractive woman in a red blazer welcomed her. Dixon took a brochure and wandered around, absorbing the cool, calm atmosphere. A hushed reverence was maintained within the building. One small alcove held flags from the homes of the men who had died within the compound. Dixon found herself wondering not about the men who had died here but about the families they had left in distant states and countries. How long had it taken them to learn that their son, husband, brother, or father would not be returning to them?

Twenty minutes later, she stepped into the blinding sunlight and made her way to the fishpond. She gazed about desperately for a white jacket. Several people were milling around the area, but not nearly as many as there were around the Alamo itself. Ignoring the fact that she had just left it, Dixon wondered what the fascination was in visiting places where so much pain and suffering had occurred.

She shook off her musings and continued to scan the group of people wandering around. There were no white jackets. Unable to remain still, she began pacing the circumference of the pond. Her nerves were dancing an erratic rhythm, and sweat plastered her shirt to her back.

It was 11:05, and still no white jacket. Maybe she had changed her mind. Dixon experienced a sharp glimmer of hope mixed with a twinge of regret at the thought. She vowed to wait until 11:15 and then leave.

The heat was becoming oppressive. She sat on the rim of the pond facing the main pathway and anxiously looked for a white jacket.

"Dixon?" Megan's surprised voice sounded behind her. "What are you doing here?"

Dixon leapt to her feet and turned, recognizing the soft, honeyed voice. Her smile died as she stared at the blinding white jacket and the blood-red carnation that Megan was wearing.

"No!" Dixon uttered a desperate denial and stepped back, her face pale as they continued to stare at each other. "Why are you here?" Dixon asked in a dry, strangled voice. *Please, let her be a tourist*, she prayed.

Megan's frown deepened. "I thought you had an appointment this morning."

"Why are you doing this?" Dixon demanded. Gloria's words began playing in her head like a stuck record: *She's been after us to introduce her for two weeks.* "You've known all along, haven't you?" she demanded. "You knew yesterday."

"Knew what?" Megan asked.

"That's why you were so eager for Gloria and Teresa to introduce you to me." Dixon felt an unexplainable anger building. What difference did it make if Megan knew? her calmer side reasoned. But the anger had gained too much momentum, and there was no stopping it now. "Why?" she asked.

"Your appointment," Megan began, but stopped. "Christ," she uttered. "It really is you I'm here to meet." She ran her hand across her mouth before she folded her arms across her body as if trying to hold herself.

"Why didn't you tell me who you were?" Dixon demanded.

"I didn't know it was you until just now. Dixon, I swear I didn't." Tears filled her eyes.

Megan was Elizabeth's descendant. Suddenly everything seemed wrong. Dixon spun and began to run. She heard Megan call after her, but she couldn't stop. Oblivious to the curious stares of those around her, she continued to run until she reached her car. With squealing tires, she tore from the parking lot and roared away from downtown. She hit the ramp to the interstate and floored the accelerator, somehow fearing if she looked up Megan would still be behind her. A car switched lanes and pulled in front of her, forcing her to slam on her brakes. She felt a stab of panic as her car slid sideways. She steered into the skid, and the car straightened out. Shaking from her near miss, she carefully left the interstate at the next exit and made her way home.

The answering machine's red eye was blinking wildly when she entered her apartment. She didn't want to talk to anyone, and she suspected the calls were from Megan. She unplugged the phone and collapsed on the sofa. How could she have been so stupid? A part of her tried to argue that Megan had done nothing wrong, but a larger, louder part told her she had been set up and used. How and why didn't matter. This was not a time for logic. She felt deeply betrayed. Why hadn't Megan told her she knew who she was all along? It wouldn't have mattered then.

She jumped at the sound of the doorbell. Mrs. Jenkins must have seen her come in. For a moment she cursed herself for helping the old woman move the chair closer to the window. She would never be able to come in again without being seen. Suddenly feeling ashamed of her own nasty thoughts, she got up. Mrs. Jenkins was lonesome and was always more than willing to help her out on a moment's notice.

Dixon opened the door and almost slammed it shut at the sight of Megan standing there. But Megan must have anticipated her slamming it. She quickly stepped forward and placed her hand on the door.

"We need to talk," she said quietly.

"How did you find me?" Dixon demanded.

"You gave me your card the other night. It had your home address," Megan replied. "May I come in?"

Had she been raging or unreasonable, Dixon could have slammed the door easily, but her quiet, almost pleading look caused her to step back and allow her to come in.

Megan closed the door behind her, and they stood in awkward silence. "Nice apartment," Megan mumbled aimlessly.

"Would you like something to drink?" Dixon asked, wondering why they now found it so difficult to talk, when it had been so easy before.

"No, thanks."

They continued to stand. Finally, Dixon motioned toward the sofa. Megan sat on the edge as if expecting to flee any moment.

Dixon sat in the recliner across from her and tried not to stare at the blood-red carnation.

Megan seemed to sense her scrutiny. She pulled the jacket off and smoothed it down beside her. "What happened back there?" Megan asked in a voice that seemed dangerously close to breaking. "Why did you run away?"

Dixon shook her head. "I'm not sure. I guess I panicked when I realized it was you I was meeting."

"Why?" Megan demanded.

Dixon shrugged. "I don't know. It seemed so . . . so . . ." What was the word she was groping for? "Incestuous," she blurted.

"Incestuous?" Megan gasped. "What in the hell are you talking about?"

Dixon wanted to get up and pace, but she was too tired to stand. "I don't know if I can explain," she began. "It's just that after the way I felt about Elizabeth, and you being a descendant . . ." She waved her hands in frustration. "Then with you deliberately trying to meet me . . ."

Megan threw up a hand and cut her off. "Whoa." A frown creased her forehead. "You've completely lost me," she declared. "Who is Elizabeth? And why were you the one I was there to meet today?"

Confused, Dixon shook her head. "Your great-great grandmother, Elizabeth Colter."

Megan's frown deepened. "Okay. I'm missing something. Let's start at the beginning. I now realize you have some connection with my family. Randolph Jackson, an attorney, called and told me he had turned over something to someone." She stopped and looked at Dixon. "After the last few minutes, I'm assuming that someone is you."

When Dixon didn't respond she continued. "Apparently he had something that had been set aside by my great-great aunt Rachel. And after he made such a fuss about it, I guess I got a little curious about what it was. When he wouldn't tell me, my curiosity got worse, and I decided I wanted to meet whoever it was behind all of this."

She shrugged as if to ask what's the big deal.

"You must know more than that," Dixon persisted. "That couldn't have been the first time you had heard of Randolph Jackson." Dixon looked at her closely. "I want . . . no, I need to know everything you know about Elizabeth and Rachel Colter."

Megan hesitated a moment. "All right." She seemed to be thinking for a moment. "I guess the best place to start is when my dad died." She scooted back on the sofa and crossed her legs. Dixon couldn't stop the spark of desire that she felt as Megan's shirt collar opened just enough to allow her a brief peek of soft, creamy cleavage.

Unaware of the effect she was having on Dixon, Megan swept back her hair and continued. "It was about a week or so after Dad's funeral," she explained. "I was getting ready to go back to California to start the process of moving my business out here, when I got a call from Dad's lawyer, Randolph Jackson." Megan stopped. "Well, he wasn't exactly Dad's lawyer. I guess he was really Mom's." She shook her head. "Sorry, I'm a little confused about that."

Dixon felt a deep sense of dread beginning.

"Anyway," Megan continued. "Mr. Jackson told me that my mother's family had kept his firm on retainer for years to handle a matter that had developed with my great-great aunt," she shrugged, "or it could have been great-great-great aunt." She looked slightly embarrassed. "I never paid much attention at the time. He told me that Dad had directed him to keep doing whatever it was he was doing, and he assured me that the financial considerations were taken care of. I was still upset over Dad's death and a little strung out about all the details with my impending business move. I more or less blew him off." She picked at some imaginary lint on her jeans.

"I'd pretty much forgot about him, and then a few weeks ago he called again and said he had opened a letter that gave him instructions on how to dispose of this item he had been holding all of those years."

She looked at Dixon and smiled. "Wouldn't that get you curious?"

Dixon nodded, unable to speak.

"My curiosity got the best of me, and I tried to pry out of him what this was about, but all he would tell me was that my great — however many times — aunt had left something that he was supposed to hand over to someone on May first."

She stopped and tilted her head slightly. "I guess I should tell you that at this point I thought he was off his rocker. I called the bar association, and they had nothing but praise for Mr. Jackson. I didn't know what to make of all this, and I had no one else to talk with. I'm what you call the last of the line."

Dixon felt the pain of Megan's last statement. She wanted to reach out and ease her pain, but she feared her touch might not be welcomed now. She shuddered at the thought of being totally alone in the world and made a mental note to call her mom later. She might be a pain sometimes, but Dixon couldn't imagine not being able to talk to her whenever she chose. She wanted to mumble her apologies or something, but her throat was too tight to allow even the smallest sound to escape. It had never occurred to her that Elizabeth's descendant wouldn't know what had happened. But it made sense now that she thought about it. How could Elizabeth have told anyone that she was from the twentieth century?

Megan was watching her. "You don't intend to make this any easier, do you?"

When Dixon looked away, Megan sighed and continued. "Basically, Mr. Jackson didn't tell me anything beyond who had retained him. He wouldn't tell me what it was, who it was for, or how the person was to receive whatever it was. A few days later, he called to tell me that the item had been given to the appropriate person and that he would make arrangements to have the trust fund that had been established to pay for the firm's services transferred over to me."

Dixon shifted, and Megan held up one hand. "Don't bother asking about the fund. I don't know anything about it."

Dixon swallowed several times before she could speak. "What about the person he met?" Dixon asked cautiously. "Didn't you wonder who your ancestors would be transferring something to?"

Megan shrugged. "I assumed it was a grant to some organization. It's not unusual for my family —" She stopped suddenly, and a guarded look crossed her face. "He said the item had been delivered to the appropriate person." Megan looked at her closely. "And as I said earlier, I guess that would have been you."

Their gazes locked for several moments. Dixon looked away first.

Megan continued. "That's when I started badgering him to introduce us. I was curious about all the secrecy."

Megan uncrossed her legs and leaned forward, resting her elbows on her knees. "I kept after him, and you finally agreed to meet me, and" — she held her hands up before letting them drop helplessly into her lap — "you know the rest."

Dixon sat frozen in place. She knew that she would have to tell Megan the truth and that she would probably lose her as a result. Jennifer had been the only person she had fully shared the entire story with, and she had not believed her. So why would Megan, when Megan hardly knew her?

"I think it's your turn," Megan prompted.

Dixon swallowed the lump in her throat. "Can we put all of this behind us and pretend we just met?" Dixon pleaded.

Megan sat quietly for a long moment. "I don't think we could build a very solid foundation for a relationship with this many secrets between us," she stated. "I would always wonder if —" She stopped. "There would be too many doubts," she finished lamely.

"Even if what I tell you drives us farther apart?" Dixon persisted.

Megan closed her eyes and rested her face in her hands. "Damn," she whispered. "I thought that maybe, just this once, it would be different."

"What would be different?" Dixon asked.

Megan shook her head. "It doesn't matter." She stood and picked up her jacket. "Why don't I leave before this gets nasty?"

Dixon frowned. "Why do you think it'll get nasty? You don't even know what I'm going to tell you."

Megan gave a sad, lopsided smile. "It may be a different version, but trust me, it all boils down to the same ending."

"Which is?" Dixon demanded, angry that she was being judged before she got to tell her side. What the hell did Megan think was going on anyway?

Megan suddenly threw her jacket back onto the sofa. "All right, damn you. Tell me your story, and let's see how original you can be." She dropped down heavily beside her jacket. "But let me warn you. You'll have to have a great story to beat some I've already heard."

Confused, Dixon started to question her, but the look on Megan's face stopped her. Dixon sat down and stared at Megan, wondering where she could begin.

"First of all, this isn't really about Rachel. It's about Elizabeth, your great-great grandmother. Rachel took care of the legal arrangements. The box was from Elizabeth. Rachel was Elizabeth's lover and was no actual blood kin to you." The look on Megan's face told Dixon that this wasn't the right opening. Flustered, she took a deep breath and started again.

"Have you ever seen a photo of your great-great grandmother, Elizabeth Colter?"

"Yes. There was an album that belonged to my grandfather and there were several photos of her in it." Megan's face was set hard as stone.

"I'll be right back," Dixon said and ran into her

bedroom to retrieve the photos and journals that Elizabeth had left her. Returning to the living room, she placed the journals on the table before Megan and handed her the photos.

She watched the color drain from Megan's face as she looked at them. "I'll give you points for originality," she spat, flinging the pictures onto the table by the journals.

Dixon gently gathered the photos and moved them to her side of the table away from Megan. She felt a streak of anger that Megan would treat the photos with such carelessness.

Megan looked at her watch. "Look, I have another appointment in less than an hour, so if you insist on continuing with this charade, then hurry up. I need to leave soon."

Scared and angry, Dixon blurted out her story, beginning with the day she had met Elizabeth and her class at the Alamo and continuing on until the meeting with Megan today at the Alamo.

Megan sat in stunned silence when Dixon finished. After what felt like an eternity, she finally shook her head. "Let me see if I've got this straight," she said softly. "You actually knew my great-great grandmother, Elizabeth Colter. The two of you went camping last year and crawled through a tunnel that took you back in time. You came back and Elizabeth died in the landslide. But somehow Elizabeth also managed to stay there, fall in love with a woman who should have been dead, had my great-grandmother Dixon, who in turn got married and had my grandfather, Mason Dixon, who in turn produced my mother, who produced me. And these" — she motioned to the journals in front of her — "are actually the life journals of Elizabeth Colter, sent to you some eighty-odd years after she died."

Dixon nodded, knowing it sounded like the ravings of a madwoman.

Megan laughed harshly, but Dixon could see the glint of tears in her eyes. She wished she could remove the pain.

"I'll say this for you," Megan said softly, "you win hands down. That's the best one I've heard yet."

"Why do you keep saying that?" Dixon asked.

Megan pretended to be shocked. "Of course, you don't know, do you?"

"Know what?" Dixon demanded, feeling her anger rising again.

Megan stood abruptly. "God, do we have to drag this out? You win. I'm the fool, okay?" She grabbed her jacket and started for the door. She stopped sharply and turned back. "Just out of curiosity, how much were you after? Or were you hoping I'd take you into my bed and heart and that you'd have everything?"

Confused, Dixon shook her head. "What are you talking about?"

For a moment a small look of hope flashed across Megan's face, but she pushed it away and shook her head. "I'm such an ass." She turned and reached for the doorknob.

"Megan, wait," Dixon pleaded. "I don't understand."

"Dixon, please." Her voice broke. "Don't make this any harder."

Dixon walked over and put her hand on Megan's arm. "Please," she begged, "don't leave. We can talk this thing through. I can prove what I'm telling you is true if you'll just hear me out."

"Why should I?" Megan demanded.

Dixon hesitated. "Because I think I'm falling in love with you."

Megan spun and grabbed Dixon. She pinned her to the entryway wall and kissed her harshly. Her teeth ground into Dixon's lips, bruising them. Dixon struggled against her, but Megan held her firmly. When Megan finally pulled away, tears streamed down her cheeks. Dixon looked away, hurt and ashamed of Megan's attack.

"What the matter?" Megan spat. "Isn't that what you were after?"

When Dixon didn't respond, Megan gave an ugly laugh. "Of course it isn't." She slid her hand into her pocket and flung something. Dixon ducked, and the metal object cut into her cheek as Megan slammed the door behind her. Dixon slid down the wall, holding her stinging cheek. The object that had struck her was a money clip with a rather thick fold of bills clamped in it. Confused, Dixon stared from the money clip to the blood on her hand.

Dixon lost track of time as she continued to sit in the entryway, trying to comprehend what had occurred between her and Megan. Somehow, from Megan's point of view, money had become involved. After several hours, the only thing that was clear to Dixon was that she wanted Megan. She admitted to herself that she loved Megan and that she would do whatever it took to make things right again. There was only one other person Dixon could turn to, and she had already told Dixon she didn't want to have anything else to do with her.

"Well, too bad," Dixon mumbled, struggling to her feet. As she stood before the bathroom mirror cleaning the cut on her face that turned out to be rather superficial, she made up her mind. Jennifer was her only hope of convincing Megan that she was telling the truth.

Dixon carefully packaged the journals and the letter from Elizabeth. Tomorrow morning she would call a courier service and have them delivered to Megan, and then she would find Jennifer and convince her to help.

Getting to Jennifer proved to be a more difficult task than Dixon had anticipated. Dixon hadn't realized how busy a downtown hospital emergency room is. She had sent two messages in to Jennifer with different nurses and was told to wait. Jennifer would see her as soon as possible. It was after 4:00 before Jennifer came out of the emergency room doors. She was dressed in her street clothes and carried a large canvas bag.

"This is still about Elizabeth, isn't it?" she asked as they stepped outside into the sweltering heat. Dixon tried to talk to her, but Jennifer held up her hand to stop her. "Yes or no?" she demanded.

"Yes," Dixon admitted meekly.

Jennifer gave a long, tired sigh. "I have to pick up two kids from school, one from guitar lessons, and then one from soccer practice. Go home, I'll get to you as soon as I can." Seeing the desperation in Dixon's eyes, Jennifer patted her arm. "I promise to be there as soon as John gets home. He can fix dinner for himself and the boys." She started to walk away, but stopped. "I've done a lot of thinking," she said, and shook her head. "I don't have time to go into it now." She rubbed her palm over her cheek and sighed. "Look, I'm starving and Elizabeth told me what a horrible cook you are, so order a pizza or something."

In an attempt to alleviate some of the guilt she felt, Dixon stopped by her favorite Italian restaurant and got a wide selection of entrées to go. If Jennifer was willing to take time to listen to her, the least she could do was feed her.

When Jennifer arrived at Dixon's apartment, a hot meal and a bottle of chilled wine were waiting for her. Jennifer sipped the wine and moaned her appreciation over the cannelloni. "If you could actually cook like this, I would divorce John and marry you," she sighed. Seeing Dixon's shocked look, she chuckled. "I was joking, Dixon. John's a wonderful cook, and he does windows."

"Sorry," Dixon said and tried to grin. She realized that to Jennifer she must seem too serious.

Jennifer started to push her barely-touched plate away. "What's wrong?"

Seeing the exhaustion in Jennifer's eyes, Dixon shook her head. "It can wait. Let's eat, and then we'll talk."

Jennifer eyed the plate hungrily. "Are you sure?"

"I'm sure," Dixon insisted.

Dixon had never noticed how long it could take to finish a meal. She almost shouted with joy when Jennifer pushed back her plate again. "All right," Jennifer began, "let's talk."

Dixon took the wine bucket with a fresh bottle of wine and insisted they go into the living room.

She hadn't realized how nervous she was until she tried to think of a way to tell Jennifer what she needed. On her third bungled attempt, Jennifer interrupted.

"I'm assuming whatever you're trying to tell me has something to do with Elizabeth?" she began.

Dixon nodded.

"I thought so." She dropped her head against the sofa back. "You're determined to make me face this whether I want to or not."

"I'm really sorry," Dixon replied, "but something has changed, and I need your help."

"What's changed?" Jennifer asked cautiously.

"I met the woman who is Elizabeth's descendant."

"Damn." Jennifer took a long drink of wine. She fidgeted with a tassel on the pillow next to her. "And?" she asked at length.

Dixon turned the glass of wine in her hand around and around. "And. I fell in love with her."

"Jesus," Jennifer sighed. "Dixon, I'm no psychologist, but this reeks of —"

"Stop it!" Dixon shouted. "I'm not crazy, and I'm not transferring my feeling for Elizabeth to Megan." She stood and began to pace. "Megan is nothing like Elizabeth. They are total opposites."

"But you loved Elizabeth," Jennifer interjected softly.

Dixon stopped and faced her. "Yes, I did. Or at least I thought I did for several years. But we worked that out when Elizabeth met Rachel. It was hard to admit, but I finally had to face the fact that I was using Elizabeth to keep from having to make a commitment to anyone else."

"I see," Jennifer said. She set her wineglass on the table beside the sofa and drew her feet beneath her.

"I really love Megan," Dixon continued.

"So what's the problem?"

"She thinks I'm nuts, and there is some kind of confusion over money." Without thinking, Dixon touched the cut on her cheek.

"Is that how you came by that?" Jennifer asked, pointing to Dixon's cheek.

Dixon felt herself blushing and nodded.

"She sounds kind of violent," Jennifer offered.

"It wasn't like that," Dixon said, defending Megan. "She didn't intend to hit me." Dixon looked directly at Jennifer. "Do you believe what I've told you about Elizabeth?"

Jennifer sat quietly for a moment. "Dixon, I have to admit that when you first told me what happened out there, I thought you were suffering from some kind of psychological trauma. After reading Elizabeth's journals, I tried to block what was staring me in the face. And when you told me a descendant of Elizabeth's was trying to contact you, it scared me. It scared me more than I want to admit. Even to myself," she added. "Something unexplainable — something that goes against everything I believe — has happened." She shook her head. "I've thought about this a lot." She took a deep breath and looked at Dixon. "I know you're telling the truth. I know that Elizabeth did somehow manage to go back in time. And I'm sorry my own weakness made you face this alone." Tears brimmed in her eyes. "Elizabeth wouldn't have wanted me to treat you the way I have. I'm sorry."

Dixon sat beside her on the sofa and took her hand. "I understand. I need your help. Will you help me convince Megan I'm telling the truth?"

Jennifer nodded. "Yes, I'll do whatever I can."

Dixon almost shouted with joy. "Great, can we go now?" Dixon started to jump up, but Jennifer grabbed her arm.

"Whoa. Not so fast. Let's start by you telling me something about this great-great niece I've suddenly acquired."

Dixon settled down beside her. "Okay. She owns a helicopter transport service. Her father recently died. She's the last surviving member of her family."

"So there's no one else?" Jennifer asked quietly. "She's all that's survived of Elizabeth and Rachel's time on earth?"

Dixon felt a touch of sadness. "No," she answered quietly. "There's us and all the friends that Elizabeth had before."

Jennifer smiled and squeezed Dixon's hand. "You're right. The wine is making me melodramatic. What do you want me to do?"

"Talk to her. Convince her I'm not making this up."

Jennifer sat quietly. "Why don't you tell me what has happened between the two of you and then we'll decide what to do."

Dixon patiently explained what had happened between her and Megan during the last few days. She didn't mention those wonderful few hours on the beach or the night in Megan's office.

After listening to all the details, Jennifer agreed to see Megan and try to talk to her. They had a long discussion before Dixon agreed it would be better if Jennifer went alone.

Jennifer stood to go. "I have to get home. I haven't seen John in three days." She gathered up her canvas bag. "I'll call Megan tomorrow," she promised, "and I'll call you as soon as I talk to her." She gave Dixon a long hug. "I'm not promising anything," she reminded her. "She still has the last word in all this."

"I know," Dixon said. "But she's bound to believe you."

Jennifer grimaced. "Let's hope so."

Unable to sleep, Dixon cleaned her apartment, did her laundry, packed a box of clothes she no longer wore, and wrote a long letter to her mom. The sun came up and since she wasn't sleepy she took Mrs. Jenkins to breakfast and helped her mop her kitchen floor. It was only a little after 2:00 in the afternoon when she returned to her apartment, still too keyed up to sleep.

Megan would have received the journals yesterday. Maybe she had read some of them or at least Elizabeth's letter to Dixon.

She tried to sleep on the sofa but kept jumping up to make sure the phone was still working. She finally gave up and began to reclean her camera equipment.

It was after 7:00 before the phone finally rang. It was Jennifer. "I'm sorry," she said bluntly.

Dixon slumped to the sofa. She had been so sure Megan would listen to Jennifer. "What happened?"

"Not much, really. I stopped by her house. She

wasn't there so I tried to catch her at work. She was out on a flight, and I had to wait around for an hour or so before she came in. When I tried to explain who I was and why I was there, she practically threw me out. I called her house and left a long message on her machine. Maybe she will at least listen to that." Jennifer gave a tired sigh. "I'm sorry."

"Don't worry about it," Dixon mumbled. "You gave it your best." She swallowed her tears. "Thanks anyway."

She hung up the phone and stared into space. The walls began to close in, and there was only one place she could think about going to. It took her less than twenty minutes to pack and slip a note under Mrs. Jenkins's door.

The following morning found her sitting atop a high ledge staring at the soaring peak of El Capitan in the Guadalupe Mountains National Park. She had lost Megan. Or maybe she had never truly had her, she reasoned. Either way she hurt, and this was the only place she could think of for the total solitude she needed.

Her breath caught as the sun climbed above the horizon and cast its first rays of gold and red across the land below. No place she had ever been affected her as strongly as these mountains. She had thought she would never be able to return after Elizabeth's death, but now that she knew Elizabeth had lived a long and love-filled life, she once again felt at ease here.

She continued to sit, soaking in the beauty, until

the scorching sun climbed high into the sky. It was hot and would get much hotter before the day was over. She walked back to her camp where she packed her backpack in preparation for a two-day hike up to the Guadalupe Peak and back through the Bowl. It was a strenuous hike, and she would have to carry a lot of water, but it was just what she needed now to clear her head. After ensuring the balance and weight of her pack was distributed, she went to the ranger station to get a trail permit. She would leave early the next morning.

After getting the permit, she returned to camp to retrieve her day pack and filled a two-gallon container with water. She headed for the trail that she and Elizabeth had been on when they found the tunnel. She didn't know what she was expecting to find, but she knew she needed to be there. She had no difficulty finding the large flat rock she had been lying on when she discovered the tunnel. She gazed up the slope where the tunnel had been; a solid limestone wall loomed before her. Dixon took off her pack, sat in the small circle of shade the rock offered, and leaned back against it. She tried to close her eyes, but Megan's face kept materializing. After several useless attempts at relaxing, she grabbed her pack and strode off to complete the rest of the hike.

She slept restlessly that night and was on the trail at the first hint of daybreak. The rough, rocky terrain demanded her full attention. Megan could only intrude when Dixon stopped to rest, so she made sure her rest breaks were few and of short duration. Only the sun's constant reminder made her stop at all. She walked longer than she should have and arrived at one of the designated camping areas late and was forced to set up the pup tent in the dark. Even though she was exhausted, sleep was long in coming. The strong winds tore at her shelter, and the rain shower that struck a little before daybreak forced her to delay her hike until the tent dried. Noon found her perched on a narrow ledge overlooking a vast, wooded canyon. As she sat staring at the spectacular view, her vision blurred with tears. For over an hour she sat crying, unable to tell herself why. When she finally stood and dried her eyes, she was ready to head back to her base camp. She knew now where she needed to be. That night she continued walking until she reached her base camp. After fixing a hot meal of dehydrated soup, she crawled into her tent and slept soundly until mid-morning when the heat drove her out. She waited until it was almost sundown before she packed her day pack with enough food and water for two days and headed toward the old stage station.

A cloud slipped away from the face of the moon, and the station's rocky skeleton loomed around her. It was now only the jumble of debris she had remembered it being. Dixon looked around, remembering how it had looked when she and Elizabeth found it. Her gaze drifted to the hilltop where the three graves were now marked by three modern-day, precisely-cut, white wooden crosses. No matter how hard Elizabeth had tried, she had changed history. There should have been four graves on the hilltop.

Dixon made her way inside the disintegrated walls and settled against a small three-foot section that continued to stand upright. She sat still, allowing her eyes to pick out shapes in the darkness. For the briefest moment she imagined she could smell the faint aroma of coffee and bacon and hear the squeaking of the rocker in which Elizabeth had sat mending the shirt on the night she had informed Dixon she had decided to remain with Rachel. Dixon removed her pack and put it on the ground beside her. She pushed away all thoughts of Megan, only allowing memories of her days spent here with Elizabeth and Rachel, where their love had begun to blossom. The steady squeak of the phantom rocker and the exertion of the past few days slowly relaxed her body, and she soon settled into a gentle slumber. Her dreams were filled with scenes of Elizabeth and Rachel's life together. Like the flickering image of old home movies, she watched Dixon Junior grow from a small bundle into a beautiful young woman. Dixon saw in her the same cool, green eyes that Elizabeth had possessed. As her dreams drifted through their lives, Dixon was consumed with a warmth and a sense of belonging that she had never known. Slowly the images changed, and rather than Elizabeth and Rachel's faces she now saw hers and Megan's. She tried to rekindle her anger at Megan's betrayal, but Megan's presence only intensified. Again she felt Megan's hands on her trembling body and Megan's mouth on her hungering lips. Demanding. Dixon felt her body responding to the soft tracings of Megan's fingers on her skin and hot breath against her neck. Megan's hands slid between Dixon's legs and plunged into her wetness.

Dixon was shaken awake by the consuming orgasm that ripped through her. She trembled from the intensity of it. As her body gradually relaxed, she stared at the stars and smiled. As the night's chill swept over her, she reached for her pack and removed a flashlight. She wouldn't need to remain here as long as she had originally thought.] She gathered her stuff and headed back to her camp. Suddenly in a hurry to get back to San Antonio and Megan, she stretched out her stride. Megan was her future, regardless of their past, and she wasn't going to give up.

The sun was up and she was practically running by the time that she reached her base camp. She pulled up sharply as she raced around the tent. Megan sat staring out at the majestic view. She didn't turn as Dixon approached her.

"I saw you at the Lesbians in Government dance," Megan said without turning. "You were so gorgeous. I couldn't stop looking at you all night, but I was too afraid to approach you. I've known Gloria and Teresa for years. I went to high school with Gloria," she explained. "When I saw you with them I decided I would get them to introduce you to me because I wanted you alone, without all those people." She continued to gaze at the view as Dixon dropped her pack and sat beside her.

"When I saw you at the Alamo," Megan continued, "I guess I thought the worst."

Dixon started to speak, but Megan held up her hand. "There's something you don't know. When I was growing up, I heard the sketchy, jumbled kind of family history that I'm sure other people hear when they're young. Stories about my parents, a few about my grandparents, none of which I knew, by the way. They died before I was born. My parents were married late. My mom was forty-two when I was born. She died when I was twenty-seven and, as I told you, Dad died about six months ago." She rubbed a hand along her arm. "My parents loved me, but we were never a really close, tell-me-everything-you-know kind of family. Does that make sense?" she asked, looking at Dixon with a frown.

Dixon nodded, and Megan continued.

"While I was settling my father's estate, I realized how much I missed living in San Antonio. I decided to move my business back. My family . . ." she hesitated. "I'm the sole heir to Rockwall Enterprises."

Dixon felt her head spin and grabbed onto an outcropping of rock to steady herself. She had recently read an article on Rockwall Enterprises. It was one of the largest companies in San Antonio, with branches all over the United States. It was famous for its generous donations and funding for education.

Megan again looked at Dixon. "Elizabeth Colter began Rockwall Enterprises."

Dixon smiled to herself, knowing why Elizabeth had decided to change one small aspect of history. Hopefully, because of her efforts, there were a few teachers out there who could now spend more hours teaching and less time trying to gather funds for supplies.

Megan's voice brought Dixon out of her musing. "I moved to California eight years ago. I left because no matter where I turned, people knew who I was. I . . . I got involved with someone who I thought really loved me." She brushed away a bug buzzing around her head. "It turned out she liked the idea of Rockwall Enterprises a lot more than she did me. When she found out I invested everything I received from the company back into it, she dumped me. I've had a couple of other similar experiences. So I guess I'm a little gun-shy now."

"I didn't know anything about Rockwall," Dixon replied.

"I know that now." She glanced at Dixon. "Jennifer is rather persistent. She showed up at my door around midnight last night, demanding that I at least listen to her."

"She has been through a lot in the last year," Dixon said. "We all have," she added.

Megan nodded. "I think you'll agree this whole thing has been rather bizarre for everyone," she whispered.

"I know," Dixon agreed.

Megan continued. "When you showed up for the meeting at the Alamo after we'd . . ." She shrugged. "I let my imagination run away with me. I wasn't prepared for the story you had to tell me, and I let all the bad things that have happened to me previously . . . I took them out on you, and I'm sorry."

Dixon reached for her hand, and when Megan didn't pull away she held it as one would a frightened bird that might take flight at any moment.

"After I talked with Jennifer, we called Randolph Jackson, and I'm afraid the two of us were rather harsh on him." She chuckled. "The poor man probably wishes he had never heard of any of us. After Jennifer explained who she was and showed him the letter you wrote giving him permission to give out information —"

"What letter?" Dixon asked.

Megan laughed. "The one Jennifer and I wrote and signed your name to, of course. After he saw that, and with a little persuasion, he told us everything he knew. I realized I hadn't been very fair to you. I went to your apartment, and finally your neighbor, Mrs. Jenkins, told me you were up here, so I flew over."

Dixon looked around.

"The park wouldn't allow me to land the helicopter here," Megan said, a slight grin playing at the corners of her mouth. "I had to land in Carlsbad and rent a car."

"I was on my way back," Dixon said, squeezing Megan's hand. "I had decided I couldn't let you go without at least another try. We have a lot to talk about."

"We have plenty of time." Megan leaned forward to meet Dixon's lips.

Publications from
BELLA BOOKS, INC.
The best in contemporary lesbian fiction

P.O. Box 10543, Tallahassee, FL 32302
Phone: 800-729-4992
www.bellabooks.com

WHEN LOVE FINDS A HOME by Megan Carter. 280 pp. What will it take for Anna and Rona to find their way back to each other again?   1-59493-041-4 $12.95

MEMORIES TO DIE FOR by Adrian Gold. 240pp. Rachel Katz, a forensic psychologist, attempts to avoid her attraction to the charms of Anna Sigurdson. Will Anna's persistence and patience get her past Rachel's fears of a broken heart?   1-59493-038-4 $12.95

SILENT HEART by Claire McNab. 280 pp. Exotic lesbian romance.
                                                            1-59493-044-9 $12.95

MIDNIGHT RAIN by Peggy J. Herring. 240 pp. Bridget McBee is determined to find the woman who saved her life.   1-59493-021-X $12.95

THE MISSING PAGE A Brenda Strange Mystery by Patty G. Henderson. 240 pp. Brenda investigates her client's murder . . .   1-59493-004-X $12.95

WHISPERS ON THE WIND by Frankie J. Jones. 240 pp. Dixon thinks she and her best friend, Elizabeth Colter, would make the perfect couple . . .   1-59493-037-6 $12.95

CALL OF THE DARK: EROTIC LESBIAN TALES OF THE SUPERNATURAL edited by Therese Szymanski—from Bella After Dark. 320 pp.   1-59493-040-6 $14.95

A TIME TO CAST AWAY A Helen Black Mystery by Pat Welch. 240 pp. Helen stops by Alice's apartment—only to find the woman dead . . .   1-59493-036-8 $12.95

DESERT OF THE HEART by Jane Rule. 224 pp. The book that launched the most popular lesbian movie of all time is back.   1-1-59493-035-X $12.95

THE NEXT WORLD by Ursula Steck. 240 pp. Anna's friend Mido is threatened and eventually disappears . . .   1-59493-024-4 $12.95

CALL SHOTGUN by Jaime Clevenger. 240 pp. Kelly gets pulled back into the world of private investigation . . .   1-59493-016-3 $12.95

52 PICKUP by Bonnie J. Morris and E.B. Casey. 240 pp. 52 hot, romantic tales—one for every Saturday night of the year.   1-59493-026-0 $12.95

GOLD FEVER by Lyn Denison. 240 pp. Kate's first love, Ashley, returns to their home town, where Kate now lives . . .   1-1-59493-039-2 $12.95

RISKY INVESTMENT by Beth Moore. 240 pp. Lynn's best friend and roommate needs her to pretend Chris is his fiancé. But nothing is ever easy.   1-59493-019-8 $12.95

HUNTER'S WAY by Gerri Hill. 240 pp. Homicide detective Tori Hunter is forced to team up with the hot-tempered Samantha Kennedy.   1-59493-018-X $12.95

CAR POOL by Karin Kallmaker. 240 pp. Soft shoulders, merging traffic and slippery when wet . . . Anthea and Shay find love in the car pool. 1-59493-013-9 $12.95

NO SISTER OF MINE by Jeanne G'Fellers. 240 pp. Telepathic women fight to coexist with a patriarchal society that wishes their eradication. ISBN 1-59493-017-1 $12.95

ON THE WINGS OF LOVE by Megan Carter. 240 pp. Stacie's reporting career is on the rocks. She has to interview bestselling author Cheryl, or else! ISBN 1-59493-027-9 $12.95

WICKED GOOD TIME by Diana Tremain Braund. 224 pp. Does Christina need Miki as a protector . . . or want her as a lover? ISBN 1-59493-031-7 $12.95

THOSE WHO WAIT by Peggy J. Herring. 240 pp. Two brilliant sisters—in love with the same woman! ISBN 1-59493-032-5 $12.95

ABBY'S PASSION by Jackie Calhoun. 240 pp. Abby's bipolar sister helps turn her world upside down, so she must decide what's most important. ISBN 1-59493-014-7 $12.95

PICTURE PERFECT by Jane Vollbrecht. 240 pp. Kate is reintroduced to Casey, the daughter of an old friend. Can they withstand Kate's career? ISBN 1-59493-015-5 $12.95

PAPERBACK ROMANCE by Karin Kallmaker. 240 pp. Carolyn falls for tall, dark and . . . female . . . in this classic lesbian romance. ISBN 1-59493-033-3 $12.95

DAWN OF CHANGE by Gerri Hill. 240 pp. Susan ran away to find peace in remote Kings Canyon—then she met Shawn . . . ISBN 1-59493-011-2 $12.95

DOWN THE RABBIT HOLE by Lynne Jamneck. 240 pp. Is a killer holding a grudge against FBI Agent Samantha Skellar? ISBN 1-59493-012-0 $12.95

SEASONS OF THE HEART by Jackie Calhoun. 240 pp. Overwhelmed, Sara saw only one way out—leaving . . . ISBN 1-59493-030-9 $12.95

TURNING THE TABLES by Jessica Thomas. 240 pp. The 2nd Alex Peres Mystery. *From ghosties and ghoulies and long leggity beasties* . . . ISBN 1-59493-009-0 $12.95

FOR EVERY SEASON by Frankie Jones. 240 pp. Andi, who is investigating a 65-year-old murder, meets Janice, a charming district attorney . . . ISBN 1-59493-010-4 $12.95

LOVE ON THE LINE by Laura DeHart Young. 240 pp. Kay leaves a younger woman behind to go on a mission to Alaska . . . will she regret it? ISBN 1-59493-008-2 $12.95

UNDER THE SOUTHERN CROSS by Claire McNab. 200 pp. Lee, an American travel agent, goes down under and meets Australian Alex, and the sparks fly under the Southern Cross. ISBN 1-59493-029-5 $12.95

SUGAR by Karin Kallmaker. 240 pp. Three women want sugar from Sugar, who can't make up her mind. ISBN 1-59493-001-5 $12.95

FALL GUY by Claire McNab. 200 pp. 16th Detective Inspector Carol Ashton Mystery. ISBN 1-59493-000-7 $12.95

ONE SUMMER NIGHT by Gerri Hill. 232 pp. Johanna swore to never fall in love again— but then she met the charming Kelly . . . ISBN 1-59493-007-4 $12.95

TALK OF THE TOWN TOO by Saxon Bennett. 181 pp. Second in the series about wild and fun loving friends. ISBN 1-931513-77-5 $12.95

LOVE SPEAKS HER NAME by Laura DeHart Young. 170 pp. Love and friendship, desire and intrigue, spark this exciting sequel to *Forever and the Night*.
ISBN 1-59493-002-3 $12.95

TO HAVE AND TO HOLD by Peggy J. Herring. 184 pp. By finally letting down her defenses, will Dorian be opening herself to a devastating betrayal?

ISBN 1-59493-005-8 $12.95

WILD THINGS by Karin Kallmaker. 228 pp. Dutiful daughter Faith has met the perfect man. There's just one problem: she's in love with his sister. ISBN 1-931513-64-3 $12.95

SHARED WINDS by Kenna White. 216 pp. Can Emma rebuild more than just Lanny's marina? ISBN 1-59493-006-6 $12.95

THE UNKNOWN MILE by Jaime Clevenger. 253 pp. Kelly's world is getting more and more complicated every moment. ISBN 1-931513-57-0 $12.95

TREASURED PAST by Linda Hill. 189 pp. A shared passion for antiques leads to love.

ISBN 1-59493-003-1 $12.95

SIERRA CITY by Gerri Hill. 284 pp. Chris and Jesse cannot deny their growing attraction . . . ISBN 1-931513-98-8 $12.95

ALL THE WRONG PLACES by Karin Kallmaker. 174 pp. Sex and the single girl—Brandy is looking for love and usually she finds it. Karin Kallmaker's first *After Dark* erotic novel.

ISBN 1-931513-76-7 $12.95

WHEN THE CORPSE LIES A Motor City Thriller by Therese Szymanski. 328 pp. Butch bad-girl Brett Higgins is used to waking up next to beautiful women she hardly knows. Problem is, this one's dead. ISBN 1-931513-74-0 $12.95

GUARDED HEARTS by Hannah Rickard. 240 pp. Someone's reminding Alyssa about her secret past, and then she becomes the suspect in a series of burglaries.

ISBN 1-931513-99-6 $12.95

ONCE MORE WITH FEELING by Peggy J. Herring. 184 pp. Lighthearted, loving, romantic adventure. ISBN 1-931513-60-0 $12.95

TANGLED AND DARK A Brenda Strange Mystery by Patty G. Henderson. 240 pp. When investigating a local death, Brenda finds two possible killers—one diagnosed with Multiple Personality Disorder. ISBN 1-931513-75-9 $12.95

WHITE LACE AND PROMISES by Peggy J. Herring. 240 pp. Maxine and Betina realize sex may not be the most important thing in their lives. ISBN 1-931513-73-2 $12.95

UNFORGETTABLE by Karin Kallmaker. 288 pp. Can Rett find love with the cheerleader who broke her heart so many years ago? ISBN 1-931513-63-5 $12.95

HIGHER GROUND by Saxon Bennett. 280 pp. A delightfully complex reflection of the successful, high society lives of a small group of women. ISBN 1-931513-69-4 $12.95

LAST CALL A Detective Franco Mystery by Baxter Clare. 240 pp. Frank overlooks all else to try to solve a cold case of two murdered children . . . ISBN 1-931513-70-8 $12.95

ONCE UPON A DYKE: NEW EXPLOITS OF FAIRY-TALE LESBIANS by Karin Kallmaker, Julia Watts, Barbara Johnson & Therese Szymanski. 320 pp. You've never read fairy tales like these before! From Bella After Dark. ISBN 1-931513-71-6 $14.95

FINEST KIND OF LOVE by Diana Tremain Braund. 224 pp. Can Molly and Carolyn stop clashing long enough to see beyond their differences? ISBN 1-931513-68-6 $12.95

DREAM LOVER by Lyn Denison. 188 pp. A soft, sensuous, romantic fantasy.

ISBN 1-931513-96-1 $12.95

NEVER SAY NEVER by Linda Hill. 224 pp. A classic love story . . . where rules aren't the only things broken. ISBN 1-931513-67-8 $12.95

PAINTED MOON by Karin Kallmaker. 214 pp. Stranded together in a snowbound cabin, Jackie and Leah's lives will never be the same.　　　ISBN 1-931513-53-8　$12.95

WIZARD OF ISIS by Jean Stewart. 240 pp. Fifth in the exciting Isis series.
　　　ISBN 1-931513-71-4　$12.95

WOMAN IN THE MIRROR by Jackie Calhoun. 216 pp. Josey learns to love again, while her niece is learning to love women for the first time.　　　ISBN 1-931513-78-3　$12.95

SUBSTITUTE FOR LOVE by Karin Kallmaker. 200 pp. When Holly and Reyna meet the combination adds up to pure passion. But what about tomorrow?　　　ISBN 1-931513-62-7　$12.95

GULF BREEZE by Gerri Hill. 288 pp. Could Carly really be the woman Pat has always been searching for?　　　ISBN 1-931513-97-X　$12.95

THE TOMSTOWN INCIDENT by Penny Hayes. 184 pp. Caught between two worlds, Eloise must make a decision that will change her life forever.　ISBN 1-931513-56-2　$12.95

MAKING UP FOR LOST TIME by Karin Kallmaker. 240 pp. Discover delicious recipes for romance by the undisputed mistress.　　　ISBN 1-931513-61-9　$12.95

THE WAY LIFE SHOULD BE by Diana Tremain Braund. 173 pp. With which woman will Jennifer find the true meaning of love?　　　ISBN 1-931513-66-X　$12.95

BACK TO BASICS: A BUTCH/FEMME ANTHOLOGY edited by Therese Szymanski— from Bella After Dark. 324 pp.　　　ISBN 1-931513-35-X　$14.95

SURVIVAL OF LOVE by Frankie J. Jones. 236 pp. What will Jody do when she falls in love with her best friend's daughter?　　　ISBN 1-931513-55-4　$12.95

LESSONS IN MURDER by Claire McNab. 184 pp. 1st Detective Inspector Carol Ashton Mystery.　　　ISBN 1-931513-65-1　$12.95

DEATH BY DEATH by Claire McNab. 167 pp. 5th Denise Cleever Thriller.
　　　ISBN 1-931513-34-1　$12.95

CAUGHT IN THE NET by Jessica Thomas. 188 pp. A wickedly observant story of mystery, danger, and love in Provincetown.　　　ISBN 1-931513-54-6　$12.95

DREAMS FOUND by Lyn Denison. Australian Riley embarks on a journey to meet her birth mother . . . and gains not just a family, but the love of her life.　ISBN 1-931513-58-9　$12.95

A MOMENT'S INDISCRETION by Peggy J. Herring. 154 pp. Jackie is torn between her better judgment and the overwhelming attraction she feels for Valerie.
　　　ISBN 1-931513-59-7　$12.95

IN EVERY PORT by Karin Kallmaker. 224 pp. Jessica has a woman in every port. Will meeting Cat change all that?　　　ISBN 1-931513-36-8　$12.95

TOUCHWOOD by Karin Kallmaker. 240 pp. Rayann loves Louisa. Louisa loves Rayann. Can the decades between their ages keep them apart?　　　ISBN 1-931513-37-6　$12.95

WATERMARK by Karin Kallmaker. 248 pp. Teresa wants a future with a woman whose heart has been frozen by loss. Sequel to *Touchwood*.　　　ISBN 1-931513-38-4　$12.95

EMBRACE IN MOTION by Karin Kallmaker. 240 pp. Has Sarah found lust or love?
　　　ISBN 1-931513-39-2　$12.95

ONE DEGREE OF SEPARATION by Karin Kallmaker. 232 pp. Sizzling small town romance between Marian, the town librarian, and the new girl from the big city.
　　　ISBN 1-931513-30-9　$12.95

CRY HAVOC A Detective Franco Mystery by Baxter Clare. 240 pp. A dead hustler with a headless rooster in his lap sends Lt. L.A. Franco headfirst against Mother Love.
ISBN 1-931513931-7 $12.95

DISTANT THUNDER by Peggy J. Herring. 294 pp. Bankrobbing drifter Cordy awakens strange new feelings in Leo in this romantic tale set in the Old West.
ISBN 1-931513-28-7 $12.95

COP OUT by Claire McNab. 216 pp. 4th Detective Inspector Carol Ashton Mystery.
ISBN 1-931513-29-5 $12.95

BLOOD LINK by Claire McNab. 159 pp. 15th Detective Inspector Carol Ashton Mystery. Is Carol unwittingly playing into a deadly plan? ISBN 1-931513-27-9 $12.95

TALK OF THE TOWN by Saxon Bennett. 239 pp. With enough beer, barbecue and B.S., anything is possible! ISBN 1-931513-18-X $12.95

MAYBE NEXT TIME by Karin Kallmaker. 256 pp. Sabrina has everything she ever wanted—except Jorie. ISBN 1-931513-26-0 $12.95

WHEN GOOD GIRLS GO BAD: A Motor City Thriller by Therese Szymanski. 230 pp. Brett, Randi, and Allie join forces to stop a serial killer. ISBN 1-931513-11-2 $12.95

A DAY TOO LONG: A Helen Black Mystery by Pat Welch. 328 pp. This time Helen's fate is in her own hands. ISBN 1-931513-22-8 $12.95

THE RED LINE OF YARMALD by Diana Rivers. 256 pp. The Hadra's only hope lies in a magical red line . . . climactic sequel to *Clouds of War*. ISBN 1-931513-23-6 $12.95

OUTSIDE THE FLOCK by Jackie Calhoun. 224 pp. Jo embraces her new love and life.
ISBN 1-931513-13-9 $12.95

LEGACY OF LOVE by Marianne K. Martin. 224 pp. Read the whole Sage Bristo story.
ISBN 1-931513-15-5 $12.95

STREET RULES: A Detective Franco Mystery by Baxter Clare. 304 pp. Gritty, fast-paced mystery with compelling Detective L.A. Franco. ISBN 1-931513-14-7 $12.95

RECOGNITION FACTOR: 4th Denise Cleever Thriller by Claire McNab. 176 pp. Denise Cleever tracks a notorious terrorist to America. ISBN 1-931513-24-4 $12.95

NORA AND LIZ by Nancy Garden. 296 pp. Lesbian romance by the author of *Annie on My Mind*. ISBN 1931513-20-1 $12.95

MIDAS TOUCH by Frankie J. Jones. 208 pp. Sandra had everything but love.
ISBN 1-931513-21-X $12.95

BEYOND ALL REASON by Peggy J. Herring. 240 pp. A romance hotter than Texas.
ISBN 1-9513-25-2 $12.95

ACCIDENTAL MURDER: 14th Detective Inspector Carol Ashton Mystery by Claire McNab. 208 pp. Carol Ashton tracks an elusive killer. ISBN 1-931513-16-3 $12.95

SEEDS OF FIRE: Tunnel of Light Trilogy, Book 2 by Karin Kallmaker writing as Laura Adams. 274 pp. In Autumn's dreams no one is who they seem. ISBN 1-931513-19-8 $12.95

DRIFTING AT THE BOTTOM OF THE WORLD by Auden Bailey. 288 pp. Beautifully written first novel set in Antarctica. ISBN 1-931513-17-1 $12.95

CLOUDS OF WAR by Diana Rivers. 288 pp. Women unite to defend Zelindar!
ISBN 1-931513-12-0 $12.95